The gunn
running

Bolan didn't wa
a three-round burst into the nearer chase car's
windshield, where the driver's head should be, and
thought he heard a strangled cry before all hell
broke loose around him.

Bolan couldn't accurately count the muzzle flashes
winking at him from behind the headlights, but he
thought that there were only five. If he was right,
if he had drawn first blood with the unlucky driver,
then he had already shaved the hostile odds by
seventeen percent.

That still left five assassins, armed and angry,
throwing down at him with everything they had.

Aolani's car would never be the same. Bullets were
raking it from grill to trunk along the driver's side,
some of them coming through the now-shattered
windows. So far, Bolan could not smell any leaking
gasoline, but that was just dumb luck. Both tires
were already deflated on the driver's side, and Bolan
knew they wouldn't leave the Punchbowl in it.

Assuming they ever left at all.

MACK BOLAN ®

The Executioner

The Executioner®
Don Pendleton's
PELE'S FIRE

A GOLD EAGLE BOOK FROM
WORLDWIDE®

TORONTO • NEW YORK • LONDON
AMSTERDAM • PARIS • SYDNEY • HAMBURG
STOCKHOLM • ATHENS • TOKYO • MILAN
MADRID • WARSAW • BUDAPEST • AUCKLAND

Recycling programs
for this product may
not exist in your area.

First edition May 2009

ISBN-13: 978-0-373-64366-0
ISBN-10:   0-373-64366-7

Special thanks and acknowledgment to
Michael Newton for his contribution to this work.

PELE'S FIRE

Printed in U.S.A.

That men do not learn very much from the lessons
of history is the most important of all the lessons that
history has to teach.

—Aldous Huxley,
1894–1963
Collected Essays

I've learned enough from history to know that some
mistakes should never be repeated. I can't change
the past, but with a little luck, I just might change
the future.

—Mack Bolan

THE
MACK BOLAN

LEGEND

Nothing less than a war could have fashioned the destiny of the man called Mack Bolan. Bolan earned the Executioner title in the jungle hell of Vietnam.

But this soldier also wore another name—Sergeant Mercy. He was so tagged because of the compassion he showed to wounded comrades-in-arms and Vietnamese civilians.

Mack Bolan's second tour of duty ended prematurely when he was given emergency leave to return home and bury his family, victims of the Mob. Then he declared a one-man war against the Mafia.

He confronted the Families head-on from coast to coast, and soon a hope of victory began to appear. But Bolan had broken society's every rule. That same society started gunning for this elusive warrior—to no avail.

So Bolan was offered amnesty to work within the system against terrorism. This time, as an employee of Uncle Sam, Bolan became Colonel John Phoenix. With a command center at Stony Man Farm in Virginia, he and his new allies—Able Team and Phoenix Force—waged relentless war on a new adversary: the KGB.

But when his one true love, April Rose, died at the hands of the Soviet terror machine, Bolan severed all ties with Establishment authority.

Now, after a lengthy lone-wolf struggle and much soul-searching, the Executioner has agreed to enter an "arm's-length" alliance with his government once more, reserving the right to pursue personal missions in his Everlasting War.

Prologue

Honolulu, Hawaii

"Here they come," Tommy Puanani said. "Everyone get ready."

"Man," his brother, Ehu, muttered from the backseat of their stolen Ford sedan, "we all been ready for the past six hours."

"Never mind that," Tommy snapped. "Just do your job."

"Yeah, yeah."

It took iron will to keep from spinning in the driver's seat and reaching for his younger brother, maybe slapping Ehu's face. But what would be the point?

Across the street and half a block downrange, six young men wearing dress, blue U.S. Navy uniforms emerged from Club Femme Nu, a strip club known for hands-on dancers.

"There's Benny, right on time," John Kainoa said, from the shotgun seat.

So far, so good, Tommy Puanani thought. The cab with Benny Makani at the wheel appeared as if from nowhere, zig-zagging through traffic on Kapiolani Boulevard to double-park in front of Club Femme Nu. The taxi was a boxy model, like a poor man's SUV, that would accommodate six passengers if none of them was claustrophobic.

One young member of the six-pack spied the cab and waved to Makani.

"Gotcha," Tommy said, as the six men jammed themselves into the seats of the taxi.

Benny Makani keyed the microphone of his dash-mounted

radio and said, "Cab 41, with six fares leaving 1673 Kapiolani Boulevard, headed for 909 Halekauwila Street." His four friends in the stolen Ford received the message via a walkie-talkie, resting on the console next to Tommy Puanani's hip.

"Exotic Nights," Kekipi Ululani said, naming the destination based on its address. It was another well-known strip club where some of the dancers provided "special services."

"Whatever," Tommy said as he fired up the Ford and nosed into the flow of traffic, following Makani's cab.

"So, where's he taking them, again?" John Kainoa asked.

"Nowhere special," Tommy answered, staying focused on the taillights of the cab a block in front of him. "We tag along, see where he stops, and jump 'em."

"These Navy SEALs know all that kung-fu shit," Kekipi Ululani said.

"I told you once already," Tommy said, "they're just plain Navy. Get it? Not everybody in the goddamned Navy is a SEAL. Besides, that's why we've got the guns."

And guns they had, for damned sure. Each of them was carrying a pistol underneath his floral shirt, for starters. Tommy Puanani had a mini-Uzi with a foot-long sound suppressor attached. His brother and Kekipi Ululani both had shotguns, 12-gauge pumps with sawed-off stocks and barrels. John Kainoa was their rifleman, packing a Chinese knockoff of the classic Russian AK-47 with a folding stock and 30-round banana magazine.

"Okay," Ululani said, sounding somewhat mollified.

"Just be damn careful with them, yeah? No shooting till I say so, or it's your head on the chopping block."

Which, in this case, was not just a figure of speech.

They trailed the taxi along Kapiolani Boulevard, eastbound, until it turned into Waialae Avenue, then southeast from there until Makani found the spot he was seeking, underneath the elevated Lunalilo Freeway.

Tommy wondered if the *haole* sailors recognized their peril, even now. He guessed they were too drunk and horny to concern themselves with street signs or directions. In any case, it was too late to second-guess their driver as the Ford pulled in behind the taxi with its high beams on.

"Remember what I told you," Tommy cautioned his companions. "No one fires a shot until I do."

The sailors were unloading as Tommy stepped out of the Ford. They were confused and getting angry now, but Makani had them covered with an automatic pistol, barking at them to undress. The sailors began to argue, but the sight of four more men with firearms changed their minds, and they reluctantly complied.

It was an awkward business, stripping, when they'd had so much to drink. Their stumbling progress made Tommy Puanani nervous, but he hid it for the others' sake. When the six uniforms were piled up on the asphalt, Makani gathered them and ran them over to the Ford.

"How 'bout you let us keep our Skivvies?" asked one of the now-sober sailors.

"No problem," Tommy said, and squeezed the mini-Uzi's trigger, raking them from left to right and back again, his thirty rounds expended in three seconds.

His companions fired, as well, the heavy shotgun blasts, the automatic rifle stuttering and Makani's pistol.

Five seconds, maybe six, and it was over. Six young sailors were as old as they would ever be.

"All right," Tommy said. "Put them in the cab. We'll follow Benny out to Makapu'u and torch it there." And as an afterthought he added, "Good work, my brothers. We are on our way."

1

Leia Aolani was nervous. All right, she'd admit it—and who wouldn't be, in the same circumstances? Still, she prided herself on maintaining a measure of cool, unlike some people she could mention.

The man seated beside her in the Datsun Maxima, for instance.

Mano Polunu wasn't just nervous. He was twitching like someone about to collapse into a seizure. His head swiveled constantly, eyes scoping.

They sat parked outside the Royal Mausoleum State Monument's wrought-iron fence, with gold crowns surmounting each fencepost. Inside the fence lay buried all but two of Hawaii's ancient kings and queens, missing only King Lunalilo—who was planted at the Kawaiaha'o Church, in downtown Honolulu—and Kamehameha the Great, who'd been buried secretly in 1819, to prevent *haole* invaders from defiling his corpse.

All that death, and more to come.

But Aolani still thought they were on a mission for life.

Twitchy Polunu didn't seem so sure.

"He's late," Polunu said, glancing at his watch for something like the third time in a minute. "I believe he's late, don't you?"

"The timing was approximate," she once again reminded him. "He's flying in from the mainland, remember. Could be flight delays, who knows? Then, once he's on the ground, he has to get his bags and grab a rental car. Cut him some slack. We're cool."

"You think so, eh? We don't even know who this guy is."

"Polunu, I see the same things you see. Normal traffic on

the street, and empty spaces in the parking lot. I don't see any snipers in the bushes, and I *don't* hear any bullets whistling around our heads."

"You never hear the shot that kills you," Polunu answered.

"Thanks for that, okay? Is it possible for you to chill out just a little? Turn the heebie-jeebies down a notch or two? For my sake?"

"I don't think so, but I'll try," he said. "It's just that I keep thinking—"

"That they'll find you. Right, I get it. And I grant you, it's a real concern. That's why we're here, Polunu, remember? We need help to end this thing and keep you safe. To keep Hawaii safe."

"But we're exposed out here. You see that, right?"

"See it? I planned it, Polunu. But what I don't see is anybody sneaking up to kill you."

"Us," he said, correcting her. "It's not just me, now. You're marked, too."

That made Aolani shudder a bit, despite the warm evening. "All the more reason to follow through and finish this," she replied. "If we don't get it right the first time, we won't have a second chance."

"Because they're killers."

"Damn it, I know that!" she snapped at him. "Will you stop harping on the obvious?"

"Sorry." He didn't sound it, not even a little bit.

They sat in silence for a while, listening to traffic sounds and watching cars glide past on Nu'uanu Avenue. None turned into the parking lot. Why should they, since the mausoleum was closed for the night?

Aolani began to wonder about the other two cars in the lot, parked side by side, some twenty yards away. She'd driven past them when they entered, and both had seemed unoccupied, but there could be gunmen lying on the seats for all she knew.

Get real, she told herself.

Nobody could have known where she and Polunu had been going when they left her flat that evening, not unless he leaked the word himself. Unthinkable. He was afraid to show his face outside, much less invite his would-be killers to a meeting with the man who—Aolani hoped, at least—would stop their so-called revolution in its tracks.

"You want some gum?" she asked Polunu.

"No, thanks. It'll make me more nervous."

Aolani opened her purse and reached inside, touching the can of pepper spray that was wedged between her wallet and hairbrush. She felt a little better, knowing it was there—but not by much. It would offer no defense against a gun.

What did she really know about gunfighting anyway? Hell, or any kind of fighting, for that matter?

Whole lot of nothing, Aolani thought, and shut her purse.

"No gum?"

"Forgot I need to buy some," she replied distractedly.

He's not late, Aolani told herself. Allow for flight delays, airport security, slow baggage claim, a lineup for the rental car, the Honolulu traffic.

So, chill.

If the men who wanted Polunu dead knew where they were, she and her jittery companion would be toast by now.

Also, the odds against a random hit team cruising Honolulu's streets and spotting them outside the Royal Mausoleum by accident were astronomical. Next to impossible, she thought.

Next to, but no guarantees.

The tension made her crave a cigarette, even though she'd quit smoking eighteen months ago.

Damn you, Polunu, she thought. If we get out of this alive, I just might murder you myself.

THERE IS NO "Five-O" in Hawaii. No Jack Lord with perfect hair. In fact, no state police by any name. Still, Bolan watched his speed as he drove into Honolulu on Kamehameha Highway, not wanting attention from a traffic cop, then switched up to Nimitz Highway for a while. He also watched his rearview mirror to make sure he wasn't followed.

He thought about the contacts he'd been sent to meet and wished that he could fill in some of the blank spots that he'd found in their respective dossiers, which Hal Brognola had given to him. One was a revolutionary who had bailed out on his former comrades in Pele's Fire, an island terrorist group, when the going got too rough for his aesthetic taste. His name was Mano Polunu. The other, Leia Aolani, was supposed to be "a nationalist home-rule moderate." Polunu reached out to Aolani for help after his desertion, telling her Pele's Fire was planning something big in the next few days. Aolani in turn reached out to a fellow moderate who had contacts in the FBI.

Both Aolani and Polunu, apparently, held strong views on the subject of Hawaii's link to the United States. As Bolan understood the wrangle, which had carried on from sometime in the late eighteenth or early nineteenth century, a portion of Hawaii's native Polynesian population wanted more emphasis on native culture and religion, more influence in the state government, physical secession from the U.S.A. or some combination of the former, as yet to be agreed upon.

As usual, whenever issues of the sort aroused strong feelings, there were armed extremists who would hear no voices and no viewpoints other than their own. Bolan had seen the same phenomenon in Scotland, Northern Ireland, Asia, Africa, Latin America and even in parts of the United States.

Get half a dozen zealots in a room, then hand them guns and watch the bloodletting begin. It never failed.

Hard times had come to the Aloha State, but Bolan hoped that he could stop the action short of an all-out catastrophe.

It didn't trouble Bolan, going in without liaison to the FBI, Homeland Security or local law enforcement. All of them had jobs to do, but none were quite in Bolan's line—or else, wouldn't admit it, if they were.

Bolan required no writs or warrants, analyzed no evidence in antiseptic labs, reviewed no testimony.

And, in general, he took no prisoners.

As for the allies he had yet to meet, Bolan devoutly hoped that they could do their part, pull their own weight. He'd have enough to think about, without adopting any nursemaid's chores along the way.

The fact that one of his Hawaiian contacts was a woman didn't bother Bolan in the least. He'd fought beside some female warriors he respected, loved a couple of them and could think of one or two who might've kicked his ass.

He was almost there, a few more blocks remaining until he saw his contacts in the flesh, instead of hidden-camera photos that had caught them unawares.

Expect the worst, hope for the best.

And maybe, this time, harsh reality would fall somewhere between the two.

"WE OUGHTA TAKE HIM NOW," Ehu Puanani said.

"No," his brother, Tommy, said. "They're waiting for somebody, and I want to find out who it is."

"What fucking difference does it make?" Ehu demanded.

"Stop and think a minute, will you, Ehu, just this once? Suppose they're talking to the cops or FBI. You wanna know about it in advance, or just be taken by surprise when they bust down your door?"

Ehu sat sulking, fiddling with his shotgun, but at least he kept it down below the dashboard, so that Tommy didn't have to scold him a second time.

From the stolen Audi's backseat, Billy Maka Nani asked, "You think they're really talking to the Feds? I mean, that's gonna ruin everything, you know?"

"Not necessarily," Tommy Puanani said. "Depends on how much they already spilled, and whether they've got any evidence to back it up."

"Last time I looked, the *Haole*-Homeland gang wasn't so worried about evidence. They lock you up without a charge and send you off to someplace where you get tortured, and then the courts say you're an enemy combatant, so it doesn't matter, anyway."

"We are," Tommy Puanani said. "Enemy combatants is exactly what we are."

"Is that some kinda consolation when they fasten the electrodes on your balls?"

"Forget that chickenshit," Ehu said. "When the smoke clears, *haole* bastards will be kissing up to us and asking what *we* want, instead of telling us the way things gotta be."

"That's right, bro," Tommy told his younger brother. "Just remember that before you jump the gun and ruin everything."

"You wanna tell me what I ruined?" Ehu challenged him.

"Nothing, so far."

"You're goddamned right."

"I plan to keep it that way, too. So follow orders like a soldier, and stop bitching all the time."

Ehu gave him a fuck-you look, but kept his mouth shut for a change. Small favors.

They had a second team on Polunu and the woman, parked across the street, behind a filling station, in a Chevy Blazer that they'd stolen from a strip mall. Changed the plates, gave it a hasty racing stripe, and they were good to go. In that car, John Kainoa had the wheel, with Ben Makani riding shotgun and Steve Pilialoha in the back. All armed and waiting for the signal to move in.

But Tommy Puanani had no desire to rumble with the FBI. Who would? His homeboys couldn't match the *haoles'* budget, damned sure couldn't match their arsenal—at least, not yet— and if it came to fighting with the Feebs, next thing he knew, they would be fighting with Marines and everybody else on Uncle Sam's payroll.

The plan they had in place was so much better, but to pull it off, they had to know if any part of it had been exposed.

Granted, Mano Polunu was a minor player when he bailed, gone yellow in the stretch, but there was no way of deciding what he might know until they could pin him down and question him. Of course, the next best thing would be to silence him forever.

But sometimes, next best wasn't good enough.

So, they would wait and see.

If Polunu and the woman met some other asshole moderates with no official status, Tommy Puanani's men could kill them, then and there. If it was cops or Feds, though, then the killing would require more delicate finesse.

But every minute Polunu spent in custody or talking to the law, the more danger he posed to everything the movement stood for, everything it might accomplish in the next few days.

With Polunu silenced, then the plan could move ahead on schedule. They could strike a blow that would be felt from Honolulu all the way to Washington, D.C.

A shot heard round the world, damn right.

The *haoles* loved that kind of shit, as long as they did all the shooting.

Tommy Puanani's ancestors had been kings before the *haole* sailors had "discovered" what they liked to call the Sandwich Islands, some 230 years ago. The native life had gone to hell since then, but it was not too late to salvage something from the ruins.

Or, at least, to pay the *haoles* back in spades for all the damage they had done, Tommy vowed.

BOLAN SLOWED on his approach to the Royal Mausoleum State Monument, scouting the grounds before he took the final action to commit himself.

There were three cars in the parking lot, two sitting off together in a corner, and the third positioned closer to the entrance of the park. Bolan saw no one in the first two vehicles, although they could've been concealed. At least two people clearly occupied the third car, facing the street and watching traffic pass.

His contacts? Or a trap?

In either case, he had to check it out. If something had been leaked and this turned out to be an ambush, he would simply have to fight his way clear of the trap, then find another angle of approach into the mission.

Bolan knew the second part would likely be more difficult. If someone on the other side knew he was in Hawaii, knew the *why* of his arrival, they'd be battened down with extra-tight security until they made their one big score.

Whatever that was.

Bolan needed his contacts to give his quest direction.

He turned into the parking lot and let the cars behind him roll on to their sundry destinations: meeting lovers, going out for dinner, to a movie, maybe heading for a second job. The normal things that Bolan hadn't done—or even had much time to think about—for years.

Inside the parking lot, he drove the long way around to check the empty-looking cars. He slowed as he drove past them, staying far enough away that he could check for man-sized shadows lying underneath.

The last car was a Datsun Maxima, an older vehicle, but in decent shape. A woman occupied the driver's seat, staring at Bolan in his rental car, while a pudgy, nervous-looking man squirmed beside her. Bolan recognized them both from photos in their dossiers, although while the man looked worse in person, the woman's snapshots hadn't done her justice.

They could still be covered, shooters huddled in the backseat, out of sight, but Bolan took a chance. Drawing the 93-R from its holster, he pulled in beside the Datsun, so that his driver's window faced the lady's.

"Leia Aolani?" he inquired.

She nodded without smiling. "Matthew Cooper?"

"Make it Matt. Mano Polunu with you, there?"

The nervous shotgun rider flinched as Bolan spoke his name. He flicked anxious eyes in the woman's direction, but she wasn't looking to see it.

"That's right," she replied. "You were briefed on the mainland?"

"Bare bones," Bolan said. "Should we talk here, or go for a ride?"

Her pink, full lips were opening to answer Bolan, when a squeal of tires behind him cut her short. Glancing at his rearview mirror, Bolan saw a black sedan tearing along North Judd Street, toward a secondary entrance to the parking lot. There were three occupants, two of them staring at the point where he and Aolani sat in their respective vehicles.

"It's time to go," Bolan said.

"Right. You follow me, and—"

"No," he interrupted her. "We either take one car or split and try to hook up later, when it's safe. Your call."

"I can't just leave my car," she said, her eyes wide and staring at the black car that was in the lot now, turning their way.

Bolan thought about it for a microsecond, knowing she was right. His rental wouldn't trace to anyone, and he could always grab another from a different agency.

"Okay," he said, his door already opening. He pocketed the rental's keys, holstered his piece and took his two bags with him as he stepped across to Aolani's car. She was already moving as he settled in the backseat, gun in hand once more.

"Have you done lots of combat driving?" Bolan asked her.

"Combat driving?"

"Right. The kind where— Watch it!"

Aolani swerved to miss the charging black sedan. Her swing was wide enough, but as they passed in opposite directions, Bolan saw a weapon thrust out of the black car's left-rear window.

Bolan ducked and saw its muzzle-flashes winking in the tropic dusk. At least three slugs tore through the Datsun's fender, rattling around inside the trunk.

"That's combat," Bolan said.

"Okay, got it! Jesus!"

Aolani stamped on the accelerator, racing toward the nearest exit from the parking lot. Bolan was sorry there'd been shooting here, which might bring the police to seize his rented car, but if they took the fight away, at least there was a chance the cops would miss this crime scene.

Maybe.

But it wouldn't matter if they died, and Bolan wasn't sold on Aolani's combat-driving skills. She knew the city, but she wasn't used to fighting for her life at high speeds behind a steering wheel.

In fact, Bolan guessed, she likely wasn't used to fighting for her life at all.

He couldn't navigate and fight at the same time, so Bolan told Aolani, "I need someplace to deal with them. Sooner's better than later. We don't want the cops involved if we can help it."

"Deal with them?" she asked him, looking wide-eyed in the Datsun's rearview mirror. "What does that mean?"

"It means I'd like all three of us to walk away from this, if possible," Bolan answered.

"Is that a gun you're holding?"

"I sure hope so."

Studying the chase car, Bolan saw another fall in line behind it, nearly sideswiping a taxi in the process. Three more guns, at least, and their pursuers had a chance to flank them now.

"We have a second chase car," Bolan told his driver. "If you're not thinking of someplace we can take them, now's the perfect time to start."

2

With Aolani driving, Bolan had no opportunity to mark the streets they followed on their winding course. A few landmarks stuck in his mind, but he was focused on the chase cars that kept pace with Aolani's Datsun, regardless of the rapid zigzag course she set.

"Where are we going?" Bolan called to Aolani from his place in the backseat.

"I'm not sure, yet," she answered, her voice cracking from the strain.

"Come up with something," he responded. "If the cops get in on this, we're done."

"I'm thinking, damn it!" Then, as if by sudden inspiration, "How about the Punchbowl?"

Bolan knew something about the Punchbowl Crater from his visits to Oahu in the past. It was the cone of an extinct volcano, used at various times for human sacrifice and tribal executions, as a rifle range for the Hawaii National Guard, as an artillery emplacement protecting Pearl Harbor and finally as a national memorial cemetery for U.S. servicemen killed in the Pacific Theater during World War II. It had been years since Bolan had visited the site himself, but he knew there were public access roads and acreage for hiking.

He supposed it would do.

"How far?" he asked Aolani.

"We're halfway there. I take Ward Avenue to Iolani west-bound, loop around to San Antonio, and there we are."

"Do it," Bolan said.

Polunu gave a little groan and settled lower in his seat.

Bolan ignored the turncoat revolutionary, instead concentrating on the mechanics of the firefight that was now unavoidable. He had one pistol and 120 rounds of ammunition against six armed men in two vehicles. He'd faced worse odds and lived, but every firefight was unique, distinct and separate from all those that went before it.

He didn't think the chase cars carried any armor, but he wouldn't know for sure until he tested them, and Bolan wasn't ready for a running battle on a public street.

If they *were* armored, he was screwed.

And if they weren't, he still faced odds of six to one, with no strategic information other than the fact that one of his assailants had an automatic weapon, probably a 9 mm.

In his worst-case scenario, the enemy would corner him and keep his head down with suppressing fire, while they encircled him and took him out. They wouldn't find it easy, but it could be done.

He needed an edge.

Six men, 120 rounds. One magazine per man, if things got truly desperate. And if it came to that, if he was still alive and on his feet after the smoke cleared, he would be in need of resupply before the mission could proceed.

It was bad timing for an ambush, but the Executioner was used to that.

The only good time for an ambush came when he was ambushing his enemies.

And maybe, in the Punchbowl, he could do exactly that.

"Here's Ward," Aolani announced. "We've got about a half mile, maybe less, till we're on Iolani Avenue."

"Just get it done," Bolan replied.

"Okay, okay!"

She wrung a bit more speed out of the Datsun, weaving in and out of evening traffic on Ward Avenue, northbound. Horns blared behind them after each maneuver, and continued bleating as the chase cars followed Aolani's lead. The second group of hunters clipped a taxi but kept going, leaving several cars behind them in a tangled snarl.

That tears it, Bolan thought. If no one had seen fit to call the cops before, a hit-and-run was sure to get them on their cell phones.

"We're running out of time," he warned Aolani.

"Doing the best I can," she said. "It's just a Datsun, not a rocket sled."

"Expect the cruisers any minute," he replied.

"We won't be here!"

Polunu moaned again and sank completely out of sight, which was the best thing he could do, if shooting started up again.

"Here's San Antonio," Aolani said, still intent on keeping Bolan posted on their progress. He said nothing, focused on the two chase cars that followed them around the loop, spiraling toward the cemetery that would have fresh corpses on its grounds before another hour was gone.

"THEY'RE HEADING for the Punchbowl," Ehu Puanani said.

"I see that," Tommy told his brother, his hands pale-knuckled where he clenched the steering wheel. His mini-Uzi rested on the seat beside him, wedged against his hip.

"I know I hit their car," Billy Maka Nani said, from the backseat.

"Well, it didn't slow them down," Tommy replied. "Next time, try shooting at the goddamned people."

"Yeah, okay." He muttered something else, as well, but Tommy Puanani didn't catch it.

The rearview mirror showed him John Kainoa keeping pace, despite his fender-bender with the taxi back on Iolani Avenue. Tommy knew it would've been the shits to lose three men in traffic, but he would have left them where they sat without a second thought.

Polunu was what mattered now, squeezing his nuts until he

told them everything he'd spilled to the police or Feds, whoever he was talking to. *And* finding out what Aolani had to do with it, since she wasn't exactly friendly with the cops.

Now, they'd picked up another player out of nowhere. Tommy didn't recognize the *haole,* but that didn't necessarily mean anything. There were a million Feds to choose from in the new police state. No one could pretend to know them all.

And if he wasn't a Fed? What, then?

The question out of left field angered Tommy, made him wish he'd never thought of it. For damned sure, there was no time to debate it with himself right now, when he had urgent, bloody work to do.

"See there? They're turning in." Ehu seemed almost giddy with excitement. "Man, I told you they were going to the Punchbowl."

"Like this road would take them someplace else," Tommy replied, determined to rain on his brother's parade.

"I'm just saying—"

"Shut up, and be ready to rock when they stop."

The Punchbowl's public access roads were laid out roughly in concentric circles. Pele's Fire had scouted the graveyard as a possible target for the main event, then rejected it on grounds that vandalizing headstones or messing with corpses seemed both petty and perverse.

Better to kill the living than disturb the dead.

The crater's three circular roads included Inner Drive, Memorial Drive and Outer Drive, arranged in the logical order. There was also Link Drive, running south to north, which earned its name by linking Inner Drive to Outer Drive.

Simple.

Unfortunately, the graveyard alone sprawled over 112 acres, and the Punchbowl proper was larger than that, leaving more than ample room for three persons to run, duck and hide.

Or to fight, if they had the guts and guns to go for it.

So, we make sure they don't get the opportunity, Tommy thought.

Hit them hard and fast, keep Polunu breathing if they could, but in the end, the most important thing was to silence him for good. If Tommy had to kill the traitor here and now, he'd find some other way to learn what information Polunu had provided to their enemies.

"Watch out! They're turning!" Ehu blurted out.

"I'm not blind, damn it!" Tommy snapped.

There were no other cars in sight, a slow night at the bone orchard. Tommy supposed there had to be caretakers or guards around the place, somewhere, but if he did his business fast enough they wouldn't be a problem.

And if they got in his way, tough shit for them.

The Datsun swung right onto Outer Drive, as if to make a loop around the outskirts of the military graveyard. Tommy knew he had to watch them closely now, stay on their tails, since they could brake and bail in seconds, scattering into the night on foot.

"Be ready if they bail," he ordered, flooring the accelerator to remain close on the Datsun's tail.

"We still want Polunu, right?" Maka Nani asked from the backseat.

"I'd prefer it," Tommy said. "But if he pulls any shit, protect yourself."

"I hear you, brah."

"I hope he has a piece," Ehu said, hunching forward with his AK-47 poking up above the dash. "I fucking hope he does."

AOLANI WISHED she knew what she was doing. Okay, driving, that was obvious, but driving for her life while men with guns tailgated her was something new and terrifying.

Something that could make her lose it, if she wasn't very careful now.

"Start looking for a place to stop," Bolan said.

"Stop what? The car?"

"And try to take them by surprise, if possible."

"Any suggestions?" she inquired sarcastically.

"When you see a likely spot, first kill your lights, then turn in without braking. Throw them off. Something like that."

She understood about the taillights and the brake lights giving her away, but with the chase car riding on her bumper, Aolani didn't think she'd be deceiving anybody with a sudden swerve.

"They'll see me, anyway," she said.

"With any luck, they'll overshoot," Bolan replied. "Buy us a few more seconds to get ready."

Ready? Sure. Ready to die.

Her only weapon was a can of pepper spray, unused since she had purchased it. Polunu, at her personal insistence, was unarmed. That gave them one gun against six or more, and Aolani didn't even know if Cooper was a decent shot.

We're dead, she thought. I may as well just drive around until I find an open grave, and jump right in.

And it was *her* fault, damn it. Had to be. The gunmen had to have followed her to Polunu's place, or had the rundown little house staked out. In either case, they'd clearly followed her to the Royal Mausoleum and waited to see who showed up. Now Cooper was at mortal risk, along with Polunu and herself.

Focus!

A place to stop.

A place to—

There!

"Hang on!" she warned her passengers, and did as Cooper had suggested—killed her lights and swung the steering wheel hard right, onto a graveled access road that pointed toward some kind of prefab shed, presumably where maintenance equipment would be stored.

Thirty or forty yards along the road, she stamped down on her brake pedal and slid the Datsun to a halt. Cooper was out and on the move before the sound of crunching gravel died, dust swirling in the headlight beams of the approaching chase cars.

"Perfect," Aolani muttered. "Now we're trapped."

"Trapped here?" Polunu was in a panic, cringing in his seat, half-crumpled to the floorboard. "Why'd you stop?"

He knew as well as she did, but his fear had taken over.

"Polunu, get out of the car!"

"They'll kill me! Kill us all!"

"You think that sitting here will save you?" she demanded. "What about the gas tank?"

"Jesus!"

That got Polunu moving, fumbling with the inside handle of his door and spilling out into the night. He left the door wide open, making Aolani reach across to slam it and kill the inner dome lights, cursing all the while.

Her car had slithered to a stop across the graveled access road, on a diagonal. Aolani was on the side nearest their rapidly approaching enemies, but fear propelled her in a leap across the Datsun's hood to cover.

Damn good thing I'm wearing slacks, she thought, and nearly laughed. Then thought, Hysteria, just what I need right now.

But what she really needed was a SWAT team or a helicopter gunship swooping in to save her from the gunmen who would surely kill her any minute now, unless some miracle occurred.

Who should she pray to, in the final moments of her life? Not Pele, since her acolytes were those about to do the killing.

Maybe Kukailimoku, the Hawaiian god of war. He'd be a good one to recruit, when bullets were about to fly—but would he save two Polynesians and a *haole* who were bent on ruining the plans of Pele's Fire?

The worst part, Aolani thought, was that she didn't even know the goddamned plan. Polunu had either kept the details to himself, or really didn't know them in the first place.

Either way, it seemed that curiosity was proving fatal once again.

BOLAN SAW Aolani roll across the Datsun's hood and drop into a crouch behind the vehicle, as high-beam headlights from the two chase cars swept their position. They had gained maybe ten seconds from the swerve off Outer Drive. One of the chase cars skidded past their turnoff, while the other nearly stalled, but both cars had them covered now, doors flying open as gunners hit the ground running.

Bolan didn't wait for them to organize. He fired a 3-round burst into the nearer chase car's windshield, where the driver's head should be, and thought he heard a strangled cry before all hell broke loose around him.

Bolan couldn't accurately count the muzzle-flashes winking at him from behind the headlights, but he thought that there were only five. If he was right, if he had drawn first blood with the unlucky driver, then he had already shaved the hostile odds by about seventeen percent.

Which still left five assassins, armed and angry, throwing down at him with everything they had.

Aolani's car would never be the same. Bullets were raking it from grille to trunk along the driver's side, some of them coming through the now shattered windows. So far, Bolan could not smell any leaking gasoline, but that was just dumb luck. Both tires were already deflated on the driver's side, and Bolan knew they wouldn't leave the Punchbowl in the Datsun.

Assuming that they ever left at all.

He wished the gun fairy had left him something more substantial in the Honolulu airport locker—possibly a compact submachine gun; better yet, some frag grenades—but he would have to work with what he had. The 93-R was a potent close-range weapon, but its Parabellum rounds could only do so much against vehicles.

But he didn't want to wreck the chase cars, anyway.

Without at least one of them functioning, he'd have to walk back to his rental car at the Royal Mausoleum.

There came a lull in firing from the other side, perhaps his enemies reloading, but he didn't trust the sudden silence. Peering cautiously around the listing tail of Aolani's Datsun, Bolan saw two shadow men breaking from cover, running to his left as if their lives depended on it.

Which they did.

Flankers, he thought, and reckoned one or two more would be making the same run off to his right, encircling Bolan's weak position. Once they faded into darkness there, they could drift back and bring him under fire, drilling their hapless targets in the back while others hiding by the chase cars kept him occupied.

But not these two.

Lying on his left side, Bolan fired twice, two 3-round bursts at moving targets twenty yards or less in front of him. It wasn't quite point-blank, but it was close enough.

The first man stumbled, clutching both arms to his chest and tumbled like a mannequin, his face slamming hard against the gravel of the access road. He shivered once or twice, then lay deathly still.

The second runner saw his comrade drop and tried to turn away from Bolan's bullets, but he didn't have that kind of speed. The bullets spun him like a novice dancer, trying out a pirouette he hasn't mastered, lurching and collapsing midway through the spin. This time, death didn't seem to be immediate, but from the spastic thrashing he observed, Bolan had no concern about his last mark rising to rejoin the fight.

He'd cut the odds by half, unless his adversaries had more men than he had counted at the onset. That was good, but Bolan had no time for self-congratulation. Rather, he assumed that one or two gunmen had flanked him on the right, while he was dealing with their comrades.

He would have to deal with them, if he intended to survive. And living on to fight another day was always part of Bolan's master plan.

He crawled to Aolani, clutched her arm and drew her close,

speaking into her ear without raising his voice. "Stay here," he said. "I'll be back soon."

"You'll be back soon?" she echoed, sounding horrified. "What are you doing, going out for coffee?"

"Just stay put!" he hissed at her. "Stay quiet, and stay down. Do that, you just might stay alive."

That said, he turned and scuttled off into the darkness.

TOMMY PUANANI SAW his brother fall, with Billy Maka Nani right behind him. Shot down, both of them, and if they weren't already dead, he guessed they would be soon.

Goddamn it! How was he supposed to tell his mother that he'd gotten little Ehu killed?

"Fuck!" he said.

"Say what?" asked Steve Pilialoha, crouched beside him in the shadow of their stolen car.

"Nothing. Did Benny make it?"

"I think so. Hard to tell, it's so damn dark out here."

Tommy had meant to send one man around in each direction—Ben Makani to his right and Billy Maka Nani to the left—flanking the three they meant to waste. But Ehu wouldn't take no for an answer, damn his stubborn ass. Not only was he set on going to the right, with Billy, but he broke from cover early, making Billy hustle to catch up.

Now both of them were dead, because his goddamned little brother was a stupid brat.

And John Kainoa, too, though that one wasn't Ehu's fault. One of the bastards they were hunting had some kind of automatic weapon, and he'd nailed John through the windshield of their second chase car right away, before John even had a chance to kill the engine.

It was idling even now, with John slumped over in the driver's seat, blood leaking from his shattered face. Just then Tommy considered what would happen if the car slipped into gear and started rolling forward. If it maybe had some help, and slammed into the bullet-riddled Datsun, for instance.

How would that be?

Pretty goddamned good.

"I've got a plan," he whispered.

"What, another one?" Pilialoha sounded skeptical.

"Shut up and listen. We can flush 'em out, we play our cards right."

"Yeah? How's that?"

"John's ride. One of us goes around to diddle the accelerator, then we give a shove, and *bam!*"

"It's not that far," Pilialoha said. "It won't be going very fast."

"Won't have to be," Tommy replied. "If the impact doesn't bring 'em out, we sit back here and shoot the shit out of the gas tank. Light 'em up."

"Sounds risky."

"Breathing's risky. Would you rather just sit here and jerk off till the cops show up?"

"No, hell, let's do it." Pilialoha paused then, frowning, and asked, "Who's rigging the gas pedal?"

"You're the mechanical genius."

"Fuck me!"

I just did, brudda, Tommy thought, but settled for, "Go on. I'll cover you."

"That's great."

While Pilialoha began duck-walking over gravel, holding his shotgun like a tightrope walker's balancing rod, Tommy pulled the nearly empty magazine from his Uzi and replaced it with a fresh one. Stuffed the almost-empty clip into his pocket, just in case he needed one more burst to finish what they'd started here, before they split.

There'd been no shooting from the Datsun since Ehu and Billy went down, but what did that mean? Tommy, enraged, had fired off half a magazine after his brother fell, but had no reason to believe that he'd hit anyone. A lucky shot, perhaps, one in a million, but he didn't really think so.

Now, he had to ask himself: who had the gun? Polunu or the *haole* stranger? Tommy couldn't picture Aolani as a threat, in terms of shooting anyone, but Polunu—while a traitor—had been trained to handle weapons.

And the *haole?* Who in hell was he?

Check his ID after he's dead, the small voice answered.

"Right."

The dome lights in the second chase car flared as Pilialoha opened the driver's door. Tommy flinched from John Kainoa's shredded face, the blood that dribbled from his chin and streaked the inside of the punctured windshield. He imagined Steve reaching for the gas pedal, between John's sagging legs.

And still no shooting from the Datsun.

Had their enemy run out of bullets? Was he waiting to find out what they'd try next?

Benny Makani hadn't fired a shot since running off into the night, so Tommy guessed he hadn't flanked their targets yet. What would they do if he just kept on running? Lost his nerve and didn't even try to take out their opponents?

"Kill him," Tommy muttered to himself. "I'll kill him nice and slow."

The second chase car's engine revved, its harsh sound startling Tommy back to the here and now. He turned and lurched off toward its trunk, prepared to do his part and set it rolling toward the enemy.

They've had it now, he thought, unconscious of the fact that he was talking to himself again.

"You've fucking had it now."

THE FLANKER WHO'D been sent to Bolan's right was on his own. Bolan had no idea what made them send two men in one direction, while another went alone, nor did he care. It was enough to know he hadn't missed a shooter in the darkness.

The guy was cautious, Bolan gave him that, but caution slowed him. A well-trained soldier would've taken half the time to cover forty yards, and likely would've been in place before Bolan was ready to receive him.

Not this guy.

A revolutionary he might be, at least in theory, but a soldier trained for war?

Not even close.

Shuffling footsteps on gravel marked his progress before Bolan saw him. The stalker carried a Kalashnikov but never had a chance to use it. The Executioner nailed him with a single shot, snapping the gunman's head back.

Easy.

When he was satisfied that no backup was coming from the shadows, Bolan closed the gap, relieved his lifeless adversary of his AK-47 and a spare clip that protruded from his pocket. Two heartbeats to check the captured rifle, and he doubled back to join his companions under fire.

And just in time.

As he arrived, one of the chase cars was accelerating toward Aolani's crippled Datsun. It wasn't going more than 20 mph by his estimate, but it would still cause damage on impact.

And it would provide cover for the last two shooters, coming up behind it while the high beams blazed their trail.

Bolan ignored the car, its lifeless driver, concentrating on the men behind it. They had revved the gas somehow, and maybe given the vehicle a shove to start, both of them clutching weapons now and sheltering behind the vehicle as it advanced. From Bolan's angle, though, one of the hunters was exposed completely, and his companion was visible from the waist up.

It was enough.

He stitched the nearer of the gunmen with a rising burst, six rounds or so of 7.62 mm death leaving the AK's muzzle at a speed of 2,300 feet per second. Downrange, his moving target crumpled as if he were made of paper, crushed within a giant's fist. The dead man fell, firing a shotgun blast into his own foot as he dropped.

The hunting party's sole survivor swung toward Bolan, ripping off a long burst from a lightweight submachine gun. Bolan could've ducked but didn't bother, instead answering with a short burst from his Kalashnikov that nearly emptied the long curved magazine.

His target took most of it, jerking through a clumsy little dance that ended with a belly flop on gravel, while the car that he'd been following rolled on and nosed against the Datsun's driver's door. It wasn't much of a collision, but it finally extinguished those annoying high beams.

Bolan advanced to find Aolani and her companion huddled on the far side of the Datsun, still staying put and keeping low. Not bad, he thought, all things considered.

She had done all right on what he took to be her first time under fire.

"It's over," Bolan said. "We need to leave now."

"Leave?" she challenged him. "In case you haven't noticed, they just shot the hell out of my car."

"We'll borrow one of theirs," Bolan replied. "That one," he added, pointing to the vehicle that stood alone now, headlights burning tunnels through the night.

"And leave mine here?"

"I'll torch it. Take out anything you need that's still inside."

As Bolan spoke, he tore a strip of fabric from a lifeless gunman's shirttail and removed the Datsun's gas cap to insert the wick.

"Burn it or not, the cops will trace it," Aolani said.

"No sweat. You're out of town right now. How could you know some punks would steal your car and use it for a rumble with a rival gang?"

"Jesus. Okay, hang on a minute, will you? Let me get my purse and—"

She was scrambling, fumbling in the glove compartment, underneath the front seat, grabbing this and that before he lit the wick. They piled into the second chase car, and he had it rolling toward the Punchbowl's exit when the Datsun blew behind them.

"This is really not what I had in mind," Aolani informed him.

"Hey, you know the saying—life's what happens while you're making other plans."

And death could happen, too.

Oh, yes.

They hadn't seen the last of death, by any means.

3

Bolan drove back to the Royal Mausoleum State Monument, avoiding major streets with Aolani's guidance. Their commandeered car was unmarked by gunfire, but Bolan didn't want to take the chance that someone had reported it along their previous route of flight. If that turned out to be the case, and once the Punchbowl slaughter was discovered, the police would soon be searching for his ride.

And Bolan planned to be long gone by that time.

They rode in silence for the most part. Bolan couldn't say for sure if Aolani was upset by all the bloodshed she had witnessed, frightened by the fact that she had nearly been among the victims, or enraged by the destruction of her Datsun. Maybe it was a bit of everything that kept her staring stiffly through the windshield, speaking only when she told him where to turn and then in husky monosyllables.

Polunu, huddled in the backseat, whimpered now and then, but otherwise stayed quiet, as if fearing what might happen if he drew attention to himself. That was fine with Bolan. Until they ditched the chase car and were back on safer wheels, he didn't need distractions that would take his mind away from here-and-now survival.

He took his time on the second approach to their starting point at the monument. He saw no evidence of any stakeout, either by police or more would-be assassins, but he hadn't seen the first ones, either.

Bolan boxed the block, then turned and did it all again, the other way around. When he was satisfied that no one lay in wait for them, he pulled into the spacious parking lot and drove directly to his rental car, parked one space over from it and got out to have a final look around.

No ambush didn't mean there was no danger.

For all Bolan knew, there could've been a third carload of hostiles watching when they fled the monument with two chase vehicles in tow. He doubted it, but stranger things had happened.

Looking over his rental car, he could see his tires weren't flat, and the locking gas cap had no signs of tampering.

What else?

He popped the hood and had a cautious look around, seeking any grim surprise package that might explode when he turned the ignition key or hit a designated speed.

Nothing.

As he prepared to look beneath the car, Aolani asked him, "What's going on? You smell a gas leak? What?"

"Just checking," Bolan said. "It won't take long."

"Checking for what?"

"For bombs," Polunu answered softly. "It's a good idea."

"Not only bombs," Bolan replied, while peering underneath the rental's fenders, moving on to check the bumpers. "We don't want to take a homer with us, either."

"Homer?" Aolani said. "What's that?"

"Tracking device," Polunu said, surprising Bolan.

He would have to judge the turncoat terrorist more carefully, see what lay underneath the mousy, terrified exterior.

"All clear, as far as I can tell," Bolan said, rising from the ground and dusting off his hands.

"As far as you can tell? That's not very encouraging," Aolani said.

"No bombs, definitely. As for homers, the technology is so advanced, I'd have to take the car apart and might not recognize it, even then. There's nothing obvious. We either take our chances as it is, or take a hike."

"They're not through hunting us, I take it?" Aolani asked.

"I doubt it," Bolan said.

"Not even close," Polunu said.

"In that case, hiking's out," Aolani replied, moving around to take the shotgun seat as Bolan sprang the latches with a button on the rental's key fob.

"Where to?" Aolani asked him, as they pulled out of the parking lot.

"Not your place," Bolan answered. "If they trailed you here, they've got you covered all the way."

"You mean I can't go home again?"

Choosing to ignore her question, Bolan said, "I want someplace where we can talk in private, without further interruption. Someplace no one would look for either one of you."

"It isn't far to Diamond Head or Kuilei Cliffs," Aolani observed. "We shouldn't have much company out there, this time of night."

"None of the wrong kind, anyway," Polunu said.

"That's southeast," Bolan said, not really asking.

"Right," Aolani agreed. "We'll pick up Kalakaua Avenue, not far ahead. Just follow it along the coast until it turns into Diamond Head Road. From there, you've got your choice of Diamond Head State Monument or Kuilei Cliffs Beach Park."

Bolan followed the course she had described, keeping a sharp eye on the rearview mirror for pursuers as he put the miles behind him. He believed it was unlikely that they'd snag another tail, but likelihood and certainty were very different things.

And there was ample room to die between the two.

The coastal route to Diamond Head was beautiful in daylight, but it had a very different quality by night. The sea beyond the nearby shore, instead of sparkling silver, blue and green, showed only shades of gray and black, highlighted by a quarter moon. It was the kind of view that made some ancient mariners believe they could set sail from home and topple off the far edge of the Earth, falling forever through a silent, airless void.

So, was it Paradise—or Limbo?

Either way, the hulk of Diamond Head was coming up in front of him, and Bolan started looking for a place to park his car.

"ALL RIGHT," Bolan said, when he'd found a dark place to park well back from the highway. "We're breathing, but there are six men dead so far, and I still don't know what in hell is going on. Somebody bring me up to speed. Right now."

Aolani turned in her seat and spoke to Polunu.

"Okay, it's my story," Polunu said.

"Let's hear it," Bolan ordered.

"How far back should I go?"

"As far back as it takes," Bolan replied.

"I'll skip the childhood shit, if that's okay with you. Or even if it's not." The tight look of defiance on his face was Bolan's first hint that the turncoat had a backbone.

"Fair enough."

"Okay. I grew up hating *haoles*. No offense, you having saved my life and all, but this is me. I hate the way you—they—take everything for granted when they spend only a few days on the islands. Leave their trash all over, put the make on native girls like they were Captain Cook, going where no man's been before. Laugh at the stupid Polynesians with their funny hair and clothes. You know?"

"I hear you."

"Yeah, you hear me, but you haven't lived it. Anyway, a friend of mine—name's not important—told me all about this group that's gonna turn the clock back. Maybe turn it forward to a better day, depending how you look at things. The guys who organized it called it Pele's Fire."

"A home-rule group," Bolan said.

"Home rule's part of it," Polunu said, "but we have groups like that all over. Talk and talk is all they do, until I'm sick of hearing it. Get off your flabby ass and do something, okay? Now, Pele's Fire, they're doers. Absolutely."

"I'm aware of certain bombings, things along that line," Bolan said.

"Sure. Why not? You *haoles* killed the red men and enslaved the blacks, then set them 'free' and segregated them until they couldn't take a piss without permission from the government. Stole half of Mexico, and now you bitch about the 'wetbacks' sneaking back into their own homeland. Locked up the Nisei in the Big War, when they had no more connection to Japan than you do. All to steal their homes and land. *Haoles* need to take their lumps for a while. I still think that."

"Which begs the question—"

"Right. Why did I split? Why am I here, right now, talking to you?"

"Exactly."

"*Haoles* need a lesson, man. I still believe that. If they left the islands overnight, I wouldn't miss a one of them. But getting rid of *haoles* doesn't take some mass destruction deal, you know?"

"Not yet," Bolan replied. "You haven't told me what they're planning."

"That's the thing, okay? I don't know what they're cooking up, exactly, but I've heard enough to know it's too damned big. Like catastrophic big, okay? And not just for the *haoles*. Man, I'm talking wasteland, here."

"That's pretty vague," Bolan said.

"Don't I know it? When you start to hear this shit, you shrug it off at first, or you go along and say it's cool. But when you start to ask around, like I did, for the details, they look at you like you've picked up the *haole* smell. Know what I mean?"

"I get the drift," Bolan replied.

"So, when this friend of mine who brought me into Pele's Fire comes up one day and tells me, 'Polunu, Joey Lanakila thinks you might be working for the Man,' I know it's time to bail, okay? I got no future in the revolution, anymore."

"So, all you have is talk about the outfit planning 'something big'?"

"Not all. Did I say all?"

"If you've got any kind of lead for me, this is the time to spit it out," Bolan said. "Or you can take it to your grave."

"Is that a threat, *haole?*"

"No need. Your own guys want you dead. You want to play dumb, we can say goodbye right now, and you can take your chances on the street."

"Hang on a minute. Shit! You heard about the missing *haole* sailors, I suppose?"

"Go on."

"Six of them, I was told."

"I'm listening."

"They're dead, okay? I give you that," Polunu said. "I wasn't in on it, but word still gets around. May turn up someday, maybe not, but Lanakila's snatch squad got their uniforms. Don't ask me why, because I've got no frigging clue. But something stinks."

Bolan agreed with that assessment, but it still put him no closer to the solution of the riddle that confounded him. He clearly needed help that Polunu and his den mother could not provide.

"I need to make a call," he said, clearly surprising both of them. "Five minutes, give or take, and then we'll hatch a plan."

He turned to Polunu, pierced him with a cold, steely glare. "If you've omitted anything, let's have it now. Once we're in motion, second-guessing's not allowed and there'll be no do-overs."

"Man, I've told you everything I know."

"Not yet," Bolan replied with utter confidence. "When I get back, I'm going to ask for names and addresses. If you don't have them, it's *aloha* time."

He took the satellite phone and the ignition key, and left them sitting in the dark.

Washington, D.C.

THE NATION'S CAPITAL lies six time zones east of Hawaii. When Japanese dive bombers attacked the U.S. Pacific Fleet at Pearl

Harbor, just before 8:00 a.m. on Sunday, December 7, 1941, most residents of Washington, D.C., were already digesting lunch.

It came as no surprise to Hal Brognola, then, when he was roused from restless sleep by a persistent buzzing, which he recognized immediately as his private hotline.

Scooping up the cordless phone, he took it with him as he left the bedroom, padding through the darkness and avoiding obstacles with the determined skill of one who's done it countless times before.

"Brognola," he announced, when he was halfway to the stairs.

"It's me," Bolan said.

"How's the vacation going?"

"More heat than I expected right away, and heavy storms anticipated," Bolan told him, speaking cagily despite the scrambler on Brognola's telephone.

The big Fed got the message. "Are you dressed for it?"

"Not really. I may pick up an umbrella in the morning, if I find something I like. Meanwhile, there's news from Cousin Polunu."

"Oh?"

"He heard about the rowing team," Bolan went on, "but doesn't know where they've run off to. It's a group thing, as suspected, but I can't begin to guess when they'll be back in town."

"Staying away for good, you think?" Brognola asked.

"I'm guessing that's affirmative."

"And how does that impact your business on the island?"

"Still unknown. I'm thinking I should reach out to the locals. Find out what they have to say about it, when they're motivated."

"You think that's wise?"

"Looks like the only way to go, right now," Bolan replied.

"Well, you're the expert," Brognola replied. "I hope they're willing to cooperate."

"It's all a matter of persuasion."

"Right. If you need anything…"

"Not yet. They threw a welcome party for me, and we got to schmooze a bit. I'd like to pay them back with a surprise."

Brognola reckoned that meant there'd be news on CNN, within the next few hours. How many dead so far? He'd have to wait and see.

"I'll be here if you need me, anytime," Brognola said.

"I'm counting on it," Bolan said, and broke the link on his end.

Brognola checked the nearest clock and found he didn't have to be awake and on the move for three more hours yet. Whether he could go back to sleep again, after the call, was anybody's guess.

He shuffled to the kitchen, turned a small light on above the sink and took the makings for a cup of cocoa from the cupboard. It was too early for coffee, and he needed something that would calm him, not rev his overactive mind.

While he waited for the kettle to heat, Brognola thought about the intel Bolan had supplied in their brief conversation. First, the hostiles had been ready for him when he hit Oahu—or, perhaps more likely, they'd been trailing one or both of his contacts. In either case, there had been bloodshed that would have the cops and media on full alert. The weapon Brognola had managed to provide for Bolan on arrival came in handy, but it wouldn't be sufficient for his needs as Bolan forged ahead with more elaborate plans.

The worst news, he supposed, was that the missing seamen had apparently been killed, not simply snatched for ransom by the terrorists of Pele's Fire. Brognola had been half expecting it, but hoping for the best against his better judgment. Bolan couldn't say with perfect certainty that they were dead, of course, but Brognola trusted his gut instinct and was prepared to write them off.

The question now was, why had they been killed?

If they were simply targets, handy stand-ins for the federal government Pele's Fire despised, wouldn't the killers crow about their triumph, claiming credit for the kills? Why would they make the sailors disappear, and then say nothing whatsoever that would link the snatch to Pele's Fire?

It didn't track, and Brognola had learned that when things didn't track, most times it was because they didn't fit.

His water boiled, and Brognola poured it into a mug with two liberal spoonfuls of powdered cocoa. While he stirred the creamy brew, he focused on the minds behind six murders, tried to crawl inside those twisted brains.

Or, viewed another way, if secrecy was critical, why grab six men at once, when it was sure to make a headline splash. Why not pick off one at a time, over a period of weeks and months, if you were simply looking for a body count?

"Because they had something in common," Brognola said, talking to his cocoa and himself.

Now, all he had to do was find out what that common factor was.

Kuilei Cliffs Beach Park

WHILE COOPER WENT to make his phone call, Aolani turned to face Polunu, huddled in the farthest corner of the rental car's backseat.

"Polunu, did you know we were being followed to the monument tonight?"

He gaped at her in horrified surprise. "You think I set that up? Man, they were after me. If I want to die sometime, I'll go with pills, you know? Drift off to sleep and have an open casket at the funeral."

"So, how'd they find us?" Aolani challenged him.

"I don't know, damn it! Maybe they were tailing *you.* You ever stop and think of that? I never see you check the rearview when we're driving. You could have a convoy on your ass and never know it."

Aolani wondered whether that was true. But even if Polunu was correct, it still left one glaring question unanswered.

He got there first. "And anyway," he said, "if they were trailing us, why wait to make the hit? We sat there at least fifteen minutes before your *haole* friend showed up. Then they came down on us. How do we know they didn't follow him?"

Aolani didn't believe that, for several reasons. First, although she'd had a meeting set up by her government contact with Cooper at the Royal Mausoleum, Aolani knew nothing else about the stranger who had saved her life tonight. She had no idea where he was coming from, the flight he had booked, or its arrival time. In short, she knew nothing about the man except his general description and his name—which, she suspected, had been snatched out of a grab bag for her benefit.

More to the point, Aolani had spoken of the meet to no one but Polunu, and she'd told *him* nothing but the time and place where they would meet an unnamed man to ask for help.

Aolani was not the one who'd blown the meet. Polunu, conversely, might have passed on what he knew to someone else.

But why?

He had deserted Pele's Fire. His former comrades wanted him dead, likely after interrogating him with methods Aolani didn't even want to think about.

Unless it was a setup all along.

Or, what if Polunu cut a deal to save himself? He could've called someone from Pele's Fire and offered two fresh victims for the price of one. Aolani didn't suppose that she was someone Joey Lanakila or the others gave a damn about; if so, they could've killed her anytime they wanted to in Honolulu. But an agent of the hated federal government, dispatched specifically to bring them down, might be a prize that could revoke a traitor's death sentence.

"Polunu," she said, with cold steel in her voice, "if I find out you set us up—"

"You'll what?" he interrupted her. "Kill me? Lady, you'll have to get in line, and there are a lot of cats in front of you who've done wet work before."

"But they don't have you, Polunu. *I* do."

"Hey, you're sounding like we're married now. What

happened to my free will, eh? I can walk out of this thing anytime I want to."

And to prove his point, Polunu settled one hand on the inner handle of the door beside him.

"Go ahead," she said, calling his bluff. "But think about it before you split. Where will you hide from your old friends in Pele's Fire? Maybe in jail?"

"Jail! What the—"

"Face it, Polunu. You've already said enough to mark yourself as an accomplice on six counts of kidnapping and murder. Since the victims were active-duty military men, that makes it federal. And you could be judged an enemy combatant, now that I think about it. So, you have to ask yourself if you'll be locked up in the Honolulu federal building, or if they'll just ship you one-way to Guantanamo."

"You're tripping now," Polunu said.

"Am I? You know what Pele's Fire has done, and even if you don't have all the details of their next big score, you've said enough to stand trial on your own, as an accessory before the fact. You could get twenty years for that alone. Of course, you'll never serve the twenty."

"No?"

"Smart money says Lanakila finds someone to take you out before you ever get to court. Sound possible?"

"Hey, man." Polunu whipped his hand back from the door handle as it was red-hot. "I never said for sure that I was leaving. We're just being hypocritical, you know?"

"The word you're groping for is *hypothetical,*" Aolani corrected him.

"Whatever. Look, I'm doing all I can, okay?"

"So far, Polunu, it isn't good enough."

"I can't tell what I don't know, right? Your boy don't want me making shit up for the hell of it, does he?"

"You got that right," Bolan said, emerging from the darkness behind Aolani. She was startled, almost jumped out of her seat.

Cooper was as quiet as a cat, she thought. He also had a cat's reflexes and the killer instinct of a jungle predator. She was embarrassed to admire him for those traits and turned her face away as he slid into the driver's seat.

Biting her tongue, she sat and waited for the stranger to proclaim her fate.

"ALL RIGHT," BOLAN SAID, turning to face both passengers at once. "Here's what we need to do."

"Listen," Polunu interrupted, "I didn't mean that shit you heard, okay? I got nowhere to go if I bail out on you, and no one to look after me. I know all that, okay? What I mean to say is, I'm sticking."

Bolan prolonged the moment with a frown. "The only thing I heard is that you plan to tell the truth. Now, if I've picked your brain for everything you know, and you want to be on your way—"

"No, man. Hell, no. I talked that out with Aolani. We're all clear on that, okay?"

"Sounds fair to me," Bolan replied. "But be aware of one thing, Polunu."

"What's that, man?"

"You try to set us up at any time, or run out in the middle of a fight in progress, then you're nothing but another enemy as far as I'm concerned. And I'm not taking any prisoners."

"I saw that at the Punchbowl," Polunu said.

"Remember it."

"I hear you, brah."

"Okay, then. Unless you have more information on the task at hand...?"

"Nothing. I'm sorry, man. It wasn't like they took me in their confidence for the high-level shit."

"Then I need someone who would know the details, or at least the broad strokes of the master plan. Someone who's still accessible."

"Meaning they haven't disappeared?" Polunu asked to clarify.

"Meaning exactly that."

"Okay, let me think," Polunu said. "The big guys all went underground a while ago, you understand. Warrants and shit were bugging them too much to stay out in the open."

"But they still have contact points," Bolan surmised. "Ways they can keep in touch with others who aren't hiding."

"Well, sure, man. Lanakila and his number two, Eddie Nahoa, have a list of phone numbers. They can reach out to anyone they know, whenever. Maybe two, three others have the list, but they're all—"

"Underground," Bolan said, finishing the sentence for him.

"Right."

"Turn it around," Bolan replied. "What happens when somebody needs to get in touch with Lanakila or Nahoa? When it's vital, and they can't afford to wait around and hope they get a call tomorrow or next week?"

"Well, *someone* has their numbers, obviously," Polunu granted. "But it sure as hell's not me."

"How long were you inside the group, Polunu?" Bolan asked.

"All the way from the beginning," Polunu said.

"Then you know, or should know, who's most trusted by the brass. Who would *you* call, if you were still inside Pele's Fire and found out something Lanakila had to know right now? Pretend his life depends on it."

"Maybe Steve Lae'ula or Bobby Niele," Polunu said reluctantly.

"And if you had to get it right the first time?" Bolan pressed him.

"Bobby Niele. He's the one I'd call."

"Has he gone underground?" Bolan asked.

"No, not really. He lives off the grid as much as possible, but I can find him."

"Without setting off alarms," Bolan insisted.

"Shouldn't be a problem," Polunu said. "I'll just—"

"Give me his address and whatever else you know about

him," Bolan interjected. "No calls, nothing that would tip him off he's having unexpected visitors."

Polunu shrugged, then nodded, rattling off an address.

"Can you guide me there?" Bolan asked Aolani.

"Yes," she said. "But first, I need at least some vague idea of what we're doing."

"My intention," Bolan answered frankly, "is to ask him for his help."

"You're serious?"

"Yes," Bolan replied.

"I don't know who Bobby Niele is, but if he's tight with Lanakila, he won't tell you anything but seven different ways to screw yourself."

"And when he's done with that, I'll ask again," Bolan explained.

"Make him an offer that he can't refuse," she said.

"He's welcome to refuse," Bolan replied. "But if we can't reach some accommodation in a reasonable time frame, I'll require another name. And possibly another, after that. Put on your thinking cap, Polunu."

"Damn it," Aolani said. "Will we even make it through the day?"

"Some will, some won't," Bolan replied, and put the rental car in gear.

4

North Shore, Oahu

Joey Lanakila listened while his second in command, Eddie Nahoa, detailed their losses from the night's fiasco. Six men dead, one vehicle destroyed, another missing, and as far as he could tell, his hit team hadn't laid a finger on the people they were sent to kill or capture.

It was a disaster, all around.

He didn't care about the cars so much—they were stolen anyway—but losing six men at a whack was painful, when the total membership of Pele's Fire included fewer than one hundred individuals.

Six dead, including Tommy Puanani, who'd been with him almost from the start. Tommy had been one of Lanakila's finest soldiers.

Gone, now. Blown away...for what?

And, more importantly, by whom?

"So, let me get this straight," he said. "They had a fix on Polunu and this Aolani woman who's been talking to him, right?"

"That's right," Nahoa said. His worry over Lanakila's possible reaction to the news was mirrored on his face.

And he was right to worry.

Lanakila's fits of rage were legendary, both within and outside Pele's Fire. They'd landed him in jail on more than one occasion, which in turn had fueled his hatred of the *haole* law.

"And all they had to do was grab the pair of them, or waste them on the street if Tommy thought they couldn't make the snatch?"

Nahoa nodded in agreement.

"So, then, explain to me why six of ours are dead, and we don't have a goddamned thing to show for it."

Nahoa swallowed hard and said, "I've told you all we know, so far. Cops have the cars and bodies now, but our guy at the morgue confirms all six were shot. Maybe two weapons, but he's guessing. We'll get copies of the autopsy reports, soon as they're done."

"Six men shot down," Lanakila said. "Now, I grant you, some of them weren't hell on wheels, but Tommy was the best I ever saw. He never let me down before."

"First time for everything," Nahoa said, then looked as if he instantly regretted it, cringing from his own words.

"Here's what I don't get," Lanakila said, ignoring him. "This Aolani woman—what's her name, again?"

"Leia."

"Whatever. She's one of the peace-and-reason crowd on home rule. Am I right?"

"She is," Nahoa said. "We've argued tactics more than once, back in the day."

"So, what's she doing at the Punchbowl, shooting people? Can you answer that?"

This time, Nahoa shrugged. "I don't know who was shooting, Joey. All I know for sure's that Tommy and his boys got shot. Who pulled the triggers on them, hey, your guess is as good as mine."

"Polunu? You think that little turncoat chickenshit could take out Tommy Puanani and five other guys? Does that make any sense to you, Eddie?"

"Depends," Nahoa answered cautiously. "Even a rat fights if it's cornered and there's no way out. Self-preservation. You know that."

"Okay, a rat will fight, but could he *win?* I just don't see it happening with Polunu. Not with odds of six to one. No way."

"Well, if it wasn't either one of them, that means it had to be..."

"Somebody else," Lanakila said.

"Like who?"

"If I knew that, I'd have his balls for breakfast. Think about it, Eddie. Why would they be at the Punchbowl in the middle of the night."

"It didn't start there," Nahoa said. "On the radio, they talked about some kind of car chase leading up to Tommy and his people getting wasted. Cops are checking out the burned remains of the second car they found, trying to get an ID on the owner. If I had to bet, I'd say it comes back to the woman."

Lanakila rose and paced the shabby parlor of his cramped four-room apartment. Living underground was getting old.

"So, Tommy either spotted them or trailed them somewhere else, and when he made his move they led him on a crosstown chase, up to the Punchbowl. Are you with me, Eddie?"

"Sure, makes sense. Except, they were supposed to hit Polunu, not follow him around the island watching him."

"Hit him or question him and find out who, if anybody, he's been talking to about our plans. Suppose Tommy saw Polunu and the bitch meet someone else. He'd try to grab the others, too."

"Depends on who they were," Nahoa said. "I doubt he'd tackle cops out on the street, like that."

"No, Tommy wasn't stupid. But he'd go for a civilian in a heartbeat. Roll him up and grill him, find out what he wants with Polunu, then get rid of him if there was any way to do it nice and clean."

"Maybe. But someone rolled up Tommy and his boys. There wasn't nothing clean about it, what I hear."

"Two guns, you said?"

"Likely, but not for sure."

"So, now we know this friend of Polunu's came prepared."

"For what?" Nahoa asked. "He couldn't know our guys would be there. Not unless we've got a leak."

"Polunu's the only leak," Lanakila said. "And I want it plugged as soon as possible, before we lose more men, more time."

Before the squealing bastard ruined everything.

"I'll put more people on it," Nahoa told him. "But he can't spill what he doesn't know."

"He knows enough to make the cops ask questions, maybe point them in the general direction of an answer. Look, we've got a schedule here. We miss it, and the whole plan—the main event—goes to hell. It wouldn't mean a goddamned thing."

Nahoa nodded rapidly. "I hear you, Joey. I'll take care of it, just like you say. I'll send the best we've got."

"You mean, the best that we've got left."

Nahoa didn't answer that. Sometimes, silence was all that kept a man alive.

Waikiki

BOBBY NIELE LIVED on Olohana Street, in Waikiki, close to the Ala Wai Canal. It was a short drive back to Waikiki from Diamond Head, but working out the maze of one-way streets in Waikiki itself required some effort.

Bolan didn't try to rush. He had a guide, and he had time. How much time still remained was something that he wouldn't know until he'd asked Bobby Niele certain questions and obtained the answers he required.

While Bolan drove and Aolani navigated, Polunu filled them in on their intended mark. Bobby Niele was a twenty-some-thing hoodlum with arrests for auto theft, assault and other crimes when he joined Pele's Fire. He'd been suspected of a rape but never charged, because the victim wouldn't testify. The revolution had rechanneled his destructive energy. Polunu warned that he was a "badass" who would not come quietly or answer any questions put to him by *haole* kidnappers.

"The main thing," Bolan said, "is that he's close enough to Lanakila and the other brass to have a fix on what they're planning. If he's not connected at the top, don't waste my time."

"I'm telling you," Polunu replied, "Bobby's the man since Lanakila and the other guys went underground."

"Why didn't he go with them?" Aolani asked, revealing skepticism that gave Bolan hope.

"Somebody has to mind the store," Polunu explained. "The pigs—sorry—have got nothing on Bobby but old shit, from when he was out on his own. He's clean today, as far as they're concerned. At least, they can't prove anything."

Polunu's description of Niele raised a whole new line of questioning in Bolan's mind. Aside from finding out what Pele's Fire was planning as its next grand gesture, he could also likely squeeze Niele for directions to Joe Lanakila's hideaway.

When he discovered what the gang of terrorists was up to, he still had to find a way to stop them. And he wasn't sure he could accomplish that with just his sidearm and the borrowed AK-47 sitting in the rental's trunk.

"I'm going to need hardware," he told Aolani.

"What, like tools?" she asked.

"Like guns."

"More guns? How many can you use?"

"Don't ask," Polunu said from the backseat. "You can never have too many."

Bolan caught Polunu's gaze in the rearview mirror. "Are you packing?" he inquired.

"Well, no. But I was speaking generally, you understand."

"So, you'd say Lanakila's people are well armed?"

"You kidding me? What do you think? They're soldiers, man."

Not even close, Bolan thought, but he kept it to himself.

They drove west along Kuhio Avenue. They were passing Waikiki's International Market Place on their left, with Fort DeRussy somewhere up ahead.

"It's not much farther now," Polunu said. "Maybe five or six more blocks. But Bobby's street is one-way going south. You can't turn into it from Kuhio."

Instead, Bolan turned north on Kalaimoku, one block east

of his intended destination. Ala Wai, at the far end, had blessed two-way traffic. Bolan turned left when he got an opening, then left again to cruise down Olohana Street, seeking Bobby Niele's flat.

He didn't plan to stop on the first pass. This was reconnaissance, checking for lookouts on the street or anything at all that smelled like danger.

"There's his place," Polunu said, pointing to Bolan's left. "The puke-green stucco with the ratty-looking porch."

Which fairly summed it up.

Niele might not be in hiding, but he wasn't living the high life.

Bolan saw parking spaces at the curb, stopped counting when he'd ticked off five, and finished checking out the quiet residential street as he approached Kuhio Avenue once more. Most of the residents on Olohana Street appeared to be asleep, or maybe just sitting in the dark and brooding over problems that tormented them.

"Once more around," Bolan said, as he reached the intersection, turned right on Kuhio, another right on Namahana Street, and right again on Kuhio. He boxed the block, one more right turn on Olohana, homing on a stretch of empty curb no more than twenty paces from Niele's doorstep.

"Up or down?" he asked Polunu.

"Upstairs and in the back. He's got a great view of the garbage cans."

He passed the rental's key to Aolani. "If I'm not back here in fifteen minutes, or if you hear shooting, drive away and don't come back."

"But you—"

"Just do it!" Bolan said, as he stepped out into the tropic night.

North Shore, Oahu

EDDIE NAHOA SNORTED two short lines of coke, hoping the drug would clear his head. Predictably, it failed to do the trick, only adding to the agitation he already felt. On top of everything, he had to worry now that Lanakila would walk in and find him high.

Screw it.

Nahoa had a job to do. Lanakila was counting on him, claiming that the whole damned master plan's success depended on Nahoa finding Polunu and the woman who'd been hiding him since he went apeshit, bailing out on Pele's Fire and everything that he claimed to believe in.

Easy, right?

He cursed the memory of Tommy Puanani, who had found Polunu and allowed him to escape, getting himself killed in the process, so he couldn't even tell Nahoa who Polunu was meeting when they jumped him.

Thanks for nothing, man, he thought.

And where should Nahoa look for Polunu now?

Oahu was Hawaii's third-largest island, but it harbored 75 percent of the state's population, some 900,000 people in all. About 40 percent of them, more than 370,000, lived within the Honolulu city limits. How in hell did Lanakila think that anyone could just reach out and pluck Polunu from the teeming crowd?

Of course, Nahoa was covering the obvious, as Tommy had before him. He had people staking out Polunu's apartment, where he hadn't shown his ugly face in weeks. Another team was watching Aolani's place, but Nahoa knew she'd have to be an idiot to go back there, mere hours after watching six men shot to shit.

He'd checked the hospitals, hoping that one or both of them were wounded, but had come up empty there. As for the hundreds, maybe thousands of hotels, motels and rooming houses scattered all over Oahu, it would take an army just to go around and ask the managers if one of them had Polunu or the bitch under his roof.

Assuming anyone would answer in the first place, short of having guns thrust in his face.

And more attention from the cops was one thing Eddie certainly could not afford right now.

But he could still do something. Nahoa had put word out on the street, through his connections in the drug scene, that Polunu had a fat price on his head. He'd phrased it as an open contract, twenty grand for Polunu still alive and capable of speaking, half that if the bounty hunters felt obliged to snuff him. In the latter case, some proof would naturally be required.

To cover all his bets, he'd put out word on Aolani, too. No payment for the girl if she was dead, which ought to weed out any trigger-happy hunters looking for an easy buck.

Polunu had not been privy to the details of their plan for the main event, as far as Nahoa knew, and Aolani couldn't pass on what the little weasel didn't know, to start with.

He craved another couple lines of coke, but didn't dare indulge himself. The last hit had been pushing it. If Lanakila looked too closely at his pupils, Nahoa knew the shit would hit the fan for real. Drugs were taboo for Pele's soldiers, one more tool the *haoles* used to break down native peoples everywhere around the world.

But Nahoa needed *something* at a time like this.

If Lanakila couldn't understand that, then he'd damn well better not find out.

"I fight the war *my* way," Nahoa muttered to himself, pulling his cell phone from its holster on his belt.

It was past time for him to touch base with his soldiers on the street and see if they were making any progress. Nahoa knew they weren't, before he even started dialing. Knew *they* would be calling *him* if they'd learned anything. But checking up on them was part of leadership. He had to keep the spurs in, keep them moving. Make damn sure that none of them were sleeping on the job.

Because his very life depended on it.

And the revolution, too.

Waikiki

BOLAN HAD SET HIMSELF a time limit and didn't plan to miss the self-imposed deadline. His target should be unaware of danger lurking on his doorstep, but in light of earlier events, he might be on alert and ready to defend himself.

Bobby Niele's four-story apartment house was nothing special. Other than its putrid paint job, it was standard-issue for the neighborhood. A locked front door barred strangers from intruding on the tenants, but the lock surrendered quickly to the lock-pick gun Bolan carried with him everywhere.

Inside the foyer, Bolan spent a precious moment checking out the bank of small mailboxes, finding Niele's name and flat number. He had a third-floor corner, at the rear, as Polunu had described.

There was no elevator, and the stairs groaned under Bolan's weight, but he assumed the tenants came and went at varied hours. If Niele heard him coming, it would obviously make his job more difficult, but Bolan was determined to succeed.

When he reached the third floor, he took more care avoiding noise as he approached Niele's door. He softly checked the knob— a long shot, definitely—and wasn't surprised to find it locked. Palming the lock-pick gun again, he bent and listened at the door for any sound that might betray Niele's location in the flat.

What if he's out? a small voice nagged at Bolan. *What if he has company?*

Too bad.

A toilet flushed somewhere inside. Using the lock-pick gun, Bolan beat the lock in seconds flat and stepped inside. He pocketed the tool and drew his Beretta, standing ready with the bedroom doorway covered when Niele appeared, a Glock tucked underneath his belt in front.

"Your call," Bolan said. "Live or die."

"Who the fuck are you?" Niele challenged.

Bolan took a long stride closer to his enemy. "We're going

for a ride," he said. "Unless you want to try the Glock, in which case you'll be staying home."

"That's not a cop's gun," Niele said, a tremor in his voice. "I notice you're not reading me my rights."

"You don't have any," Bolan said. "Last time. You want to try the Glock, or not?"

Instead of answering, Niele raised his hands and placed them cautiously atop his head, the fingers interlaced. Bolan stepped closer, watching hands and eyes, then plucked the pistol from Niele's belt and tucked it inside his own.

"Where are we going?" Niele asked.

"Someplace we can talk in private," Bolan answered.

"Why not here?"

"Your locks don't work. We might be interrupted."

As he spoke, Bolan stepped wide around Niele, for a look into the small apartment's only bedroom. Finding no one there, he almost turned away, then saw the suitcase lying open on Niele's bed. A closer look inside revealed the young man's mobile arsenal—an Ingram MAC-10 submachine gun, a stubby Ithaca shotgun, a couple of pistols and spare magazines and boxes of loose rounds.

"You won't mind if I borrow these," Bolan said. It was not a question.

"Help yourself."

With the Kalashnikov he'd already secured, Bolan supposed he had enough hardware for the remainder of his mission, and it hadn't cost him anything. He would've liked a sniper's rifle, just to round things out, but beggars couldn't always choose.

Hoisting the heavy suitcase in his left hand, Bolan held the silenced 93-R steady in his right. He had no free hand to restrain Niele, but a close-range gunshot ought to do the job if any sudden action was required.

"We're going downstairs to the street and out," he told Niele. "There's a car waiting nearby. Feel free to rabbit if you're tired of having knees."

"You're making a mistake," Niele said. "Why don't you take the guns and split. Call it a day."

"We haven't had our talk yet," Bolan said.

"I'm not the one you're looking for. Maybe you got the wrong apartment, eh? I don't know anything."

"You know I'll shoot without a second thought if you try any sudden moves," Bolan said. "Why don't you get the door."

Niele dropped his hands and did as he was told. Bolan was half expecting him to swing the door back violently, rush down the stairs and clear the landing before Bolan drew a bead on him, but Niele played it straight.

Clever, or terrified?

Bolan supposed he'd answer the question when he began to grill Niele. When he'd found a private place, where any untoward sounds would be ignored.

Torture did not appeal to Bolan. Leaving the brutality aside, it seldom produced reliable answers. But sometimes fear of torture was enough to do the job. And if it wasn't...

Bolan had a job to do. He didn't even know the stakes yet, but he was determined to find out. Niele was the enemy, and Bolan owed him nothing but a cold hole in the ground.

They reached the street and turned toward Bolan's waiting rental car. So far, so good.

Long hours of darkness stretched in front of Bolan.

And he knew they might get darker yet.

5

Honolulu

Aolani drove the rented car, with Polunu fidgeting beside her in the shotgun seat. Behind her sat a stranger who had not been introduced, but whom she knew to be Bobby Niele, one of Lanakila's aides from Pele's Fire. Cooper himself sat in the back, behind Polunu, holding a bulky-looking pistol in his lap.

"You all have made one hell of a mistake," Niele said. "You'll never know how bad until it bites you on the ass."

A muffled grunt behind her brought Aolani's eyes to the rearview mirror, where Niele's mocking smile had been replaced by a bird's-eye view of his scalp. Doubled over in pain, he muttered something that was probably a curse.

"Shut up," Bolan advised him. "When it's time for you to talk, I'll let you know. At that time, you can answer questions or recite a farewell prayer. All clear?"

"Hey, man, fu—"

Niele didn't grunt this time. There was a blur of motion in the rearview mirror, Aolani saw Cooper lashing out with fist or elbow—she couldn't really tell—and hammering Niele's right temple. The impact drove the man's skull against the door frame, and he slumped into immediate unconsciousness.

"He's tired," Bolan said. "Better let him rest up for the main event."

Aolani returned her full attention to the traffic flowing north on Nimitz Highway, skirting downtown Honolulu, rushing on toward Chinatown.

"I'm still not crystal clear on where we're going," she said.

"Drive around the waterfront," he answered from the rear, "until we find someplace where I can have a private conversation with Niele."

"You want the Honolulu side or Sand Island?" she asked.

He considered it for several seconds. In the rearview mirror, Aolani saw Cooper close his eyes, almost as if reviewing maps he'd memorized.

"Sand Island," he replied at last. "You'll have to go around and take the parkway."

"One way on, and one way off," she told him. "If it matters."

"Shouldn't be a problem," he said, sounding relaxed. "We won't be making that much noise."

"I know a place," Aolani remarked, almost unable to believe that she was taking part in this. "It's an old bunker from the war, out on the southwest corner of the island, covering Mamala Bay. The kids have parties there, sometimes—at least, we did—but if it's clear…"

"Sounds perfect," Bolan said. "Think you can find it?"

"Yeah, sure."

She followed Nimitz Highway north, then west, and north again, until the Kapalama Military Reservation appeared on her left. Aolani turned left on Libby Street, then right on Auiki, following the base perimeter without encroaching on government land. After a half mile, she turned south again onto Sand Island Access Road.

The rest was easy. Bearing south-southeast, she held her course until the road passed over water and became Sand Island Parkway. They were on the island now, with Honolulu's neon sprawl fresh-lava bright across the width of Kapalama Basin.

Finding the 1940s bunker was a bit more challenging than Aolani had allowed. It had been nearly sixteen years since she last made the trip with other members of her high school senior class, to huddle by the embers of a dying fire, passing a bottle or a joint around, and tussling with her boyfriend of the moment.

"There ought to be an access road, somewhere along in…here!"

She spied it, overgrown with weeds, and a vestige of the old excitement shivered through her. It was mixed with something else, this time, however. Aolani thought that it had to be dread.

Aolani couldn't abide the thought of torture.

But things had changed.

Six men had tried to kill her very recently, and as she watched them die, her primary emotion was relief. Aolani was glad they'd died, instead of her. She owed Cooper her life and felt no vestige of survivor's guilt.

But that was self-defense, she thought. Torture is something else.

Maybe.

She might be worrying for nothing if Niele came around and answered Cooper's questions voluntarily. And if he didn't, well, perhaps a little suffering was necessary, to protect the people of Oahu.

Aolani drove along the unpaved road for what seemed miles and miles, but which she knew was really less than one mile overall. They started running out of island, heard the surf gnashing its teeth somewhere ahead of them, then there was nothing left but beach and the dark, looming blockhouse where she had become a woman at the tender age of seventeen.

"Well, here we are," she said, as she switched off the engine.

Memories are strange, she thought.

The bunker didn't seem to have a hint of romance left.

In fact, it looked like death.

North Shore, Oahu

JOEY LANAKILA LISTENED to the distant cell phone ring and ring, two dozen times in all before he cursed and severed the connection, hit redial and tried again.

Same goddamned thing. No answer on the line.

He paced to keep from shouting his frustration at the walls, or throwing things to vent his pent-up rage. He waited five tooth-grinding minutes, tried again and got the same result.

"God*damn* it!"

Pacing didn't help the anger now. Once more, he thought. I'll give the bastard one last chance.

He hit redial again and started counting. Four rings. Six. Eleven.

"Shit!"

He veered off course, opened the study door and stepped into the corridor beyond. "Eddie? *Eddie!* Get in here! Now!"

An answer echoed from his left, as Lanakila turned and lunged back into the room where he did his best thinking these days. There were maps on one wall, bookcases on two others, and no windows to distract him with a view of surf and palm trees. This was Lanakila's war room, part and parcel of his home away from home.

But if he couldn't reach his men outside, he might as well be trapped in an abandoned well, with no one but the worms for company.

"What's up?" Eddie Nahoa sounded breathless, as if he'd just run a marathon.

"Bobby Niele isn't answering his cell," Lanakila said.

"What? That's it?"

"He never turns it off, okay? He's not fucking allowed to turn it off. I need him, and he won't pick up," Lanakila snarled.

"So, what should I do about it?" Nahoa asked.

"Have a couple guys swing by his place and check it out. If he's at home and hasn't lost an arm, some shit like that, he needs to call me, and I mean right fucking now. If something's wrong, or he's gone, call back and tell us. Get it?"

"Got it."

While Nahoa rushed to do his bidding, Lanakila tried Niele's line once more, then gave up and pocketed his cell phone.

Niele was in trouble now, whatever had become of him. If

he was slacking in their time of greatest need, Lanakila would craft a fitting punishment and mete it out himself, at his first opportunity.

And if he wasn't slacking? What, then?

Lanakila ran down the short list of possibilities.

Niele was sick.

No good. It didn't matter if his damned appendix was about to blow, or he was in the middle of a heart attack. Job one was to let Lanakila know and get another set of eyes in place, even before he called an ambulance.

The pigs had Niele.

No. If he had been arrested, Niele would've used his one phone call to tip the Honolulu lawyer who defended Pele's Fire in court and secretly donated money to the cause. The lawyer would've tipped Lanakila before he went to visit Niele and arrange his bail.

He was dead.

Before yesterday, it would've been unlikely, but after Tommy Puanani and the rest were slaughtered at the Punchbowl, Lanakila knew anything was possible. He had no idea how anyone could link the bungled hit on Polunu back to Niele—and, in fact, he didn't know that someone had done so.

Maybe the guys who'd wasted Tommy's crew were working from a hit list. Maybe they had help from the inside.

They had Polunu.

"Son of a bitch!"

The rage that had been fading slightly, suddenly came back full force. He wanted Polunu's head. Wanted to put it in a sack and take it to the crest of Mauna Loa, where he'd pitch it down into the molten lava far below.

And now, he had to worry about *two* men in the clutches of his unknown enemy. Polunu was a traitor. He'd gone over on his own initiative, stabbed Lanakila and his other brethren in the back without a second thought.

But what about Niele?

Lanakila had no cause to doubt his loyalty, up to the moment he had fallen out of touch. Where Polunu gave off signals, acting squeamish when they planned hard moves against the *haoles,* Niele was a gung-ho soldier, only holding back because his role as Lanakila's public face demanded it.

Or, was he putting on an act?

The more he thought about it, Lanakila realized the pigs had penetrated every illegal group he'd ever heard of. No group was immune to penetration and subversion from within.

But if they'd done that, if they knew his secrets, why weren't the pigs cracking down where it mattered? Why weren't his key players in prison or dead?

They don't know yet, he thought. Or maybe they don't know enough.

And if they didn't know the final secret yet, it meant they were already too late.

Sand Island

BOLAN LIT A FIRE to drive the bunker's lurking shadows back and give Bobby Niele food for thought. He took the tire iron from his rented car and placed it on the concrete floor, with one end resting in the flames to heat.

Aolani and Polunu watched him from their neutral corners. Bolan didn't have a chair for Niele, so he kicked his legs from underneath him and pinned him to the floor. Duct tape swiftly secured Niele's arms behind his back, then bound his thrashing ankles.

Bolan dragged his trussed-up hostage to the nearest wall, bright with graffiti, and positioned him to sit upright, with legs extended.

Niele strained against his bonds and got nowhere. Angry frustration settled on his face, tinged with uncertainty when he glanced at the tire iron in the fire.

"I don't know what you want with me, but—"

"Then shut up and listen," Bolan told him, "and you'll know."

Niele thought about it for a beat or two, then closed his mouth.
Better.

"You're here tonight," Bolan said, "because you're part of
Pele's Fire. The group has an event planned that will have dire
consequences if it goes ahead. You're going to supply the
details…one way, or another."

"Why not ask your rat, there?" Niele asked, slanting a glare
toward Polunu's corner. "He's the one who sells his brothers
out, not me."

Bolan ignored the question and said, "You're in over your
head, Niele. Lanakila's hung you out to dry. He should be
sitting where you are, but you're the chump."

"Oh, yeah? I'll take that up with him, next time I see him."

"There won't be a next time, Niele," Bolan promised him.
"This is your one and only chance to put things right."

"Or, what? You'll shove that tire iron in my ear? Or up my
ass? Get to it, *haole*. You don't scare me."

Bolan turned, facing Aolani, and extended his left hand.
"Give me the car keys, please."

She blinked at him, surprised by the diversion, then
produced the keys and placed them in his hand.

"You two can wait outside," he said, including Polunu in his
glance. "Go for a walk, but don't get lost."

"What's going on?" she asked him, almost whispering.

"I need some alone time with Niele."

"Please, don't do this," Aolani pleaded.

"He's given me no choice."

Niele watched the others leave, and Bolan felt a shift in
attitude, some of the earlier bravado trickling out of him. Still,
he appeared determined to hang tough.

"That's gonna scare me, eh?" Niele said. "The rat and bitch
walk out? You'll have to do better than that, *haole*."

"I think you're right," Bolan said, as he drew his pistol,
aimed and blasted Niele's left knee into bloody pulp.

The shriek was deafening inside the bunker's echo chamber. Bolan waited for the sound to trail off into sobs before he spoke again.

"You've got a limp for life, now. Maybe need a cane to get around, but still no wheelchair. Yet."

"You fucking bastard!"

Anger was expected. Bolan let it pass.

"If I had more time, Niele, I could use finesse. But as it is…" He lifted the Beretta, framed the right knee in his sights.

"You'll never stop them, man," Niele wailed. "You're too late. Get it? Nothing you can do will stop it now."

"Stop what?" asked Bolan.

"Pele's Fire!" Niele answered, and it seemed that he was smiling more than weeping now. "Fire from the sea, you prick. Nowhere to run. Nowhere to hide."

"Explain," Bolan said.

"Surf's up, motherfucker!" Niele said, and then began to bash his skull against the bunker's wall with all the strength remaining to him. He administered three solid blows before Bolan could reach him, wobbling on the fourth even before Bolan secured a handful of his hair.

Blood spilled out of Niele's mouth, and Bolan saw his jaws working with grim determination, gnawing his own tongue.

"Nurf's up," he said, grinning with bloody teeth through crimsoned lips.

Bolan stepped back, and shot Niele once more, through the forehead. The gnashing of teeth immediately stilled.

Surf's up. Fire from the sea.

What did it mean, if anything?

Bolan stepped back, holstered his piece and wrapped a handkerchief around his hand before he took the tire iron from the fire. He set it on the bunker's windowsill to cool and studied Niele's corpse.

That's discipline, he thought, with something close to grudging admiration.

But the question still remained: had Niele simply tried to put him off, or were his final words a clue to what was planned by Pele's Fire?

One thing was crystal clear.

Bolan would have to ask somebody else.

Waikiki

"WHAT THE HELL is this about?" Tom Palanaka asked.

George Inaki, riding in the Chevy Blazer's shotgun seat while Lawrence Kilenowuka drove, half turned toward the backseat and said, "You know as much as we do, man. Niele isn't answering his phone."

Palanaka hissed through his teeth and shook his head. "Guy doesn't take a call, so we're out on the street at half-past one o'clock, driving to Waikiki."

"You got a date or something? Want me to call Eddie up and tell him you're too busy for a simple job?"

"Hey, brudda, don't you be putting words in my mouth," Palanaka replied.

Palanaka was pissed at being turned out in the middle of the night for a trivial errand, but Inaki wondered if it might be something more.

"Remember what went down at the Punchbowl with Tommy Puanani and his crew," Inaki said. "I think Eddie suspects it might be something else like that."

"Oh, man," Kilenowuka said. "You mean that? There was *six* of them got wasted. Why's he only sending three of us to check out Niele's place?"

"Because it may be nothing," Inaki said. "Probably it's nothing. We're supposed to have a look around the place, is all. Find out if Bobby's home, and if he is, tell him to answer his goddamn phone, whatever. If he's gone, we phone it in. Case closed."

"And if he's dead?" Palanaka asked.

"Then we phone *that* in. Find out what we're supposed to do with him."

Coming from Honolulu, they drove east on Kalikaua Avenue, then followed Kuhio when it branched off to parallel the Ala Wai Canal. Niele's street was one of those that intersected Kuhio.

Which one?

Inaki took a scrap of paper from his pocket, keyed the Blazer's map light and refreshed his memory. "Four-sixty Olohana Street," he said.

"It's coming up," Kilenowuka told him. Then, "Shit, it's a one-way. Hang on, while I go around the block."

Kilenowuka took them north on Kalaimoku, sticking to the posted residential speed limit, giving his passengers a chance to scan parked cars and darkened porches, anywhere an ambush might be laid. Inaki saw nothing that made him think they might be wandering into a trap.

So far, at least.

A left turn onto Ala Wai Boulevard, then left again one block later, onto Niele's street. Kilenowuka slowed way down on Olohana, barely creeping, like a driver looking for an address that he'd never visited before.

Perfect.

Inaki had a Colt Python revolver in his hand, a solid piece of iron loaded with six .357 Magnum hollowpoint rounds. It wasn't high tech, but it never jammed, and if he shot somebody with it, you could guarantee the prick was going down.

Behind him, Tom Palanaka pulled a stubby riot shotgun from the gym bag at his feet and racked the slide.

"Easy with that," Inaki said.

"It's not my first time, brudda."

"No one said you were a virgin, man. Just keep your finger off the trigger less you have a target."

"It's all good."

Asshole, Inaki thought.

"Four-sixty, up there on the left," Kilenowuka said.

"I see it. Park as close by as you can," Inaki said.

"We've got a space almost in front."

"Good deal."

Kilenowuka parked the Blazer, killed the lights, but left the engine running. "Just in case we have to bail out in a hurry," he explained.

Inaki didn't argue with him. "One way or another, we'll be quick," he said. And then, to Palanaka, "Can you hide that scattergun?"

"No problem, man."

"Do it."

Palanaka shoved the shotgun down inside his pants somehow, and his stride was almost normal as they crossed the sidewalk and a little strip of grass, climbing some concrete steps to reach the porch of the green apartment house.

The front door wasn't locked, a lucky break. Inaki led the way into a small lobby, then upstairs to the third floor, northwest corner of the house. He'd never visited Niele's place before, but knew the layout from Nahoa's brief description, when he'd briefed Inaki on the mission.

"Let's be careful with the door, in case he's jumpy," he told Palanaka.

"Right."

Inaki knocked softly first, then harder.

Nothing.

Finally, he tried the knob and was surprised to feel it turn. Drawing his Colt, he shouldered through the entryway and scanned the empty living room.

"Check out the rest," he ordered Palanaka, moving slowly through the living room and kitchen, seeking anything that might turn out to be a clue.

"Nothing," Palanaka informed Inaki moments later. "No one here."

"No sign of any struggle, shit like that?"

"More nothing."

"All right, then. I'll call it in from the road. Somebody else's problem, now."

But Inaki knew that wasn't true.

If anyone in Pele's Fire had problems, this close to the day—the main event—they'd be his problems soon enough.

AOLANI STOOD beside the rented car, well back from the bunker where Bobby Niele was hog-tied with duct tape. There had been shouting—well, screaming—a short while earlier, but it had swiftly been suppressed. No further noise since then, and Aolani hoped it stayed that way.

She didn't want to know what might be going on in that man-made cave to make Niele spill his secrets, but her imagination simply made things worse. She thought about the tire iron, heating on an open fire, and flashed on gruesome things she'd studied in a class about Medieval European history.

What am I doing here?

She knew the answer to that question.

Polunu had approached her with a plea for help, begging, in fact, for her to help him thwart a catastrophic plan devised by Pele's Fire. She had been leery when he couldn't tell her any details of the plan, but his sincerity—his terror—had seemed real enough.

Aolani had contacts that extremists couldn't cultivate, including one who had agreed to listen when she shared Polunu's tale. The man had made some calls and told her that an agent would be coming to discuss the problem. Could she meet him at a certain time and place, with Polunu ready to explain himself?

She could.

And it had almost cost her her life.

Almost.

In fact, she wasn't dead. But six men were—or twelve, if Polunu was correct about the missing soldiers. Six already, and how many more to go?

"Bobby won't tell him anything," Polunu said, standing with his arms crossed as if warding off a chill, although the night was clear and warm.

"I hope you're wrong," Aolani replied. She didn't want to play this scene again, perhaps repeatedly, until Cooper found a pigeon who would sing.

As if on cue, a scuffing sound of footsteps drew her eyes back toward the bunker. Cooper stood before the entrance, rising from the stooped crouch that was necessary to pass through the doorway. After all these years, it still surprised Aolani that army engineers had built the bunker's entryway as if for dwarves.

She saw the tire iron dangling from his left hand, then swiftly turned her eyes back toward his face. Despite her curiosity, she willed him to speak first.

"He stonewalled," Polunu said, not bothering to whisper.

"Not exactly." He crossed the sand to reach them, fishing in his pocket for the rental's key. "He said, 'Surf's up. Fire from the sea.' Mean anything to either one of you?"

Polunu considered it, closing his eyes as if to scan some inner monitor, then opened them again and shook his head. "Nothing," he said.

"No idea," Aolani answered. She was not a part of Pele's Fire, had never heard of Bobby Niele before that grim night. How could she know what any of his cryptic comments were supposed to mean?

Bolan opened the trunk, replaced the tire iron in its slot, and closed the lid again. He did not look back toward the bunker, or appear to give its occupant a thought.

"So, do we take him home?" Aolani asked.

"He is home," Bolan replied. "I'll find a pay phone back in town and tell the cops where they can pick him up."

She didn't ask him if Niele was alive. The answer seemed too obvious.

So, seven dead and counting, with no end in sight.

"'Surf's up,' you said? 'Fire from the sea'?"

Bolan turned toward her, frowning. "Right. What of it?"

Aolani shrugged. "I'm not sure," she replied. "But I know someone who might have a clue. No promises, but maybe. I'm surprised I didn't think of him before."

6

North Shore, Oahu

Bolan followed Aolani's directions as they left Sand Island, taking the Moanakuna Freeway north-northwest until it merged with Highway 1. That got them past Pearl Harbor, then the six-lane blacktop split, and Bolan followed Highway 2 as it rolled north, dividing the western one-third of Oahu from the eastern two-thirds.

They drove through towns and settlements, between looming mountain ranges, the Koolau to their right, or east, the smaller Waianae off to their left, or west. It was the quickest route to Oahu's famous North Shore, bypassing all the coastal scenery of Pokai Bay, Makaha, Mokuleia, and the rest of it. Barring an ambush, they should pick up Highway 99 and follow it to meet Kamehameha Highway, south of Waimea Bay.

"All right," Bolan said, when they'd been a good half hour on the road and put Bobby Niele well behind them. "Tell me more about this character we're on our way to see."

"You got it right the first time," Aolani answered. "He's a character, like something from a movie or a novel. His name is Ron Johnson. Just a surfer, at first glance. The beach-bum type, you know? But once you really get to know him, there's a lot more to it."

"Such as?" Bolan prodded.

"Well, for one thing, he's spent his twenties and most of his thirties roaming all over the world. I personally think he was some kind of spy or mercenary, but he won't talk about it."

Marvelous, Bolan thought. He's a spy, a mercenary or a beach bum. Maybe all of the above.

"Aolani…"

"Okay, I know what you're about to say," she interrupted him. "It sounds like bullshit, right?"

"Well, since you mention it—"

"I know. And that's what I thought, too. Like, maybe he was spinning yarns to impress me."

"Leia, we can't draft people as we go along and hope they don't get killed—or get us killed."

"Don't worry about Ron. He definitely takes care of himself."

"I heard of him," Polunu said from the backseat. "An older guy, *haole,* but tough. Cops tried to bust him up one time, he took down six or seven of them by himself."

"I've heard that story, too," Aolani said. "And another time I saw him fight two guys. It wasn't his idea, you understand. They called him out while he was drinking with some friends, myself among them. He tried everything to talk them out of it, offered to buy them each a drink, but they kept pushing. When they grabbed him, well, a second, maybe two, and both of them were out cold, on the floor."

"So, he knows martial arts," Bolan replied. "That doesn't mean that he can tell us what we need to know. Polunu was inside Pele's Fire, and he can't help us. This old friend of yours—"

"Ron Johnson," she reminded him.

"Whatever. He has no ties to the group or any of its operations that you know of. We have no reason to think that he can tell us anything we don't already know."

"But he knows people," Aolani countered. "Not just surfers, either, but all kinds of people. Radicals and straights, police and criminals. You name it, he's in touch."

"Sounds like your average police informer," Bolan said.

"Just wait until you meet him. See what you think then."

Their highway joined Kamehameha, and he turned right, following the North Shore with the vast Pacific on his left. Behind the Koolau Range, pale dawn was breaking in the east.

Bolan had driven through the night and still had no idea where he was going.

"Waimea's coming up," he said. "Where do we find this man of mystery?"

"The beach," Aolani replied. "He's always on the water at sunrise."

Waimea Bay— *red water,* in Hawaiian—is one of the most famous surfing spots on Earth. Immortalized in the Beach Boys' songs, along with Pupukea's Banzai Pipeline, it drew athletes and their hangers-on from every corner of the globe for organized tournaments, or one-on-one confrontations with Nature.

But few surfers dared the red water at dawn.

When Bolan found a sandy space and parked his rented car, there were exactly two boards on the slate-gray sea offshore. The hardy aquanauts maintained a distance of two hundred yards or so between themselves, prone on their boards and waiting for the perfect ride.

It came at last. Both paddled out to meet it, lurching to their feet, and one immediately tumbled back into the rising sea. The other stood his ground, crouching slightly, and started in toward shore.

"That's Ron," Aolani said, standing close enough to brush Bolan's left elbow. "Here he comes."

"HE'S GONE? That's all you have to say? He's gone?"

Joey Lanakila clutched his cell phone almost tightly enough to crush it, while he listened to the answer from his man in Waikiki.

"I don't know what else I can tell you," George Inaki said. "We found his door unlocked, but nothing out of place to suggest any kind of fight. No pigs hanging around the area. No neighbors peeking out, like there'd been any *pilikia* in the house. No trouble, man. No Niele."

"Shit! Well, was his car there?"

Inaki hesitated. "I don't know. Nobody told us what he drives."

"Goddamn it!"

"We can double back and have another look right now. Just tell me what—"

"Forget about it. Go on home."

"Look, boss—"

He severed the connection, fuming. Lanakila didn't know what kind of car Niele drove, and couldn't think of anyone to ask.

Screw it.

After the slaughter at the Punchbowl, it was safer to assume the worst and be prepared for whatever might happen next.

But how was he supposed to do that, when he still had no idea who was tormenting him?

Okay, six dead for sure, and seven now, if he assumed Niele had been picked off by his unknown enemy. Whoever was responsible, he couldn't blame the pigs. Police or Feds would crow about it on the TV news if they'd killed Tommy Puanani and his crew. They might not air it right away, if they had put Niele in a cell, but he had rights and would've called Lanakila's lawyer instantly.

Unless he was another rat.

That thought, that possibility, froze Lanakila in his tracks. He stood with fists clenched at his sides and felt the blood rush to his head, wondering if he was about to have a stroke.

Niele, a goddamned rat?

No, he decided, and resumed his frantic pacing. That was impossible.

He knew Niele too well, had grown up with him, and would trust him with his life.

In fact, he'd done exactly that.

But if I'm wrong...

More reason, then, to track him down, if he was still alive, and find out what he had to say.

Lanakila was on the verge of bellowing for Eddie Nahoa, when he knocked and entered without waiting to be asked.

"Joey," Nahoa said, "we got a call just now."

"About?"

"Bobby."

"He called here?"

"No, sir, but we found him. That is, the police have found him."

"The police?"

"He's dead," Nahoa explained. "Somebody called the pigs, no names, and sent them to Sand Island. They found Bobby tied with duct tape. Someone shot him in the knee and in the head. That's all we know, right now."

Lanakila felt a wave of pure relief wash over him.

His old friend hadn't screwed him, hadn't sold him out. The pigs were still no closer to defeating Pele's Fire than they had been at this time yesterday.

"This comes from who? That stringer at the *Advertiser?*"

Nahoa shook his head and said, "This is our girl inside the ME's office. We'll have more when they're done cutting Bobby open."

"Doesn't matter how he died," Lanakila said. "What matters is that somebody questioned him. And if he lost a knee, maybe he spilled something besides his blood, before they capped him."

"I don't know. Bobby was pretty tough."

"Tough? Shit. We all have breaking points," Lanakila said. "Anyone who says he can hold out forever is a goddamned liar."

"So, what do we do?" Nahoa asked.

"What can we do? We're underground already, hiding like a bunch of gophers."

"Well, we could postpone the main event, or even move it up. Surprise them, either way, if they know anything about it."

"Absolutely not! No fucking way! We've worked too long for this, and I won't spoil it now, when we're so close. Changing the target date would ruin everything. We lose the symbolism, lose the major targets—"

Lanakila realized he was ranting. Stepping back a pace from

Nahoa, he recovered, swallowed hard, and said again, "No way. No goddamned way."

"Okay, man."

"What we *do,*" Lanakila said, "is find Polunu and the woman. No more half-assed measures. I want everybody on the street except our strike team and their bodyguards. Nobody else gets any sleep, has anything to eat, or stops to take a goddamned piss until those two are in the bag. You understand me? And when I say everybody, that includes you."

"Absolutely. I'll get on it now."

"You do that."

A sense of desperation settled over Lanakila. They were coming down to the wire, and he was afraid that the plan would unravel before he could score the great victory planned for the cause. Another day would do it for him, just a few more hours added to the oppression that generations of Lanakila's people had already suffered from the *haoles*.

In a moment—literally, in a flash—all that would be avenged.

But Lanakila couldn't score a touchdown if his people never made it to the one-yard line.

Polunu and Aolani could be made to talk, of that he had no doubt.

Waimea Bay

RON JOHNSON WAS a muscular six-footer who looked to weigh about 190 pounds soaking wet—which, in this case, he was. He came out of the ocean smiling at Aolani, carrying his long surfboard as if it weighed nothing. Foam trailed from his footsteps, rushing back into the sea as he approached.

As Johnson got closer, Bolan noted two small, puckered scars on the man's upper chest, left of the midline, where he'd either taken bullets or been stabbed with something like a tent peg. Lower down, a long pale scar dipped from his navel, out of sight inside his baggy swimming trunks. The rough scar on his left leg, near the shin, might be a burn or something caused by high-speed dragging over rough concrete.

Clearly, he was a man who'd been around.

But where? In what capacity?

Some kind of spy or mercenary, Aolani had suggested. Maybe bits of both.

Or maybe something else entirely.

Aolani greeted Johnson warmly, standing on tiptoes to brush his damp cheek with her lips. She stepped back, then, and made the introductions. Bolan found the surfer's handshake firm and strong, without any attempt to crush his knuckles for the hell of it.

Polunu bobbed his head and muttered something unintelligible while Johnson pumped his hand.

"So, what brings you to the beach at dawn?" Johnson asked.

They had agreed to share a version of the truth with Johnson. Aolani had explained that he already knew of Pele's Fire and disapproved of their excesses, while espousing a live-and-let-live attitude. That suited Bolan fine, since he was seeking information, not a front-line battle ally.

Aolani briefly filled him in on what they knew: the Navy kidnappings, the Punchbowl firefight. These were things Johnson would've picked up from the nightly news without connecting them. She left Bobby Niele out of it, but introduced Polunu as a defector from the group whose knowledge of the big plan was not extensive enough for their needs.

"And who are you?" Johnson asked Bolan. "Other than the strong-and-silent type?"

"Call me a troubleshooter," Bolan answered.

"Out of D.C.?"

"There, and other places."

Johnson nodded, not quite smiling now. "I shot some trouble, in my time," he said. His fingers rose to touch the round scars on his chest. "Trouble shot me. I called it even and retired."

"We're not recruiting," Bolan told him. "Leia thought you might have access to some information that would help us, maybe point us to another source. Nobody's asking you to go back in the field."

"The field," Johnson said, and his crooked smile was back. "I always loved the way they made it sound like some kind of sporting event. You ever think about that, Mr. Cooper?"

"Lately, I'm too busy," Bolan said.

"I'll bet you are. The world's a goddamned crazy place these days. Trouble needs shooting everywhere."

"I take it one place at a time."

"That helps, I guess. So, you need what from me, again?"

"We have a critical event approaching, on an unknown short-term deadline. We still need to know the what, the when and the where. Directors of the target group are underground. Our inside source is compromised and dated, with respect to locators. We need a new one."

"Even if he doesn't feel like helping you?"

"I'll reason with him," Bolan answered.

That made Johnson laugh. "Sweet reason. I remember that." His eyes turned flinty-hard and ocean-dark as he asked Bolan, "What's your plan for dealing with this problem if you work it out in time?"

"If intervention's necessary," Bolan said, "I intervene."

"With these two?" Johnson almost smirked at him.

"No. Not if I can help it."

Aolani blinked at Bolan, saying, "Hey!" Polunu looked relieved.

"I've heard that Pele's Fire has something like a hundred guys," Johnson said.

"Then they're down to ninety-three," Bolan replied.

"Uh-huh. But odds catch up with you, don't they?"

"It happens," Bolan granted.

"See, my problem is, this is my home. I wasn't born here,

but I chose it, which is even better. This is where and how I choose to live, after too many years playing the big boys' game, out in *the field*."

"I told you, we're not—"

"Looking for recruits, I know. I heard you. But if Pele's Fire has something cooking that will spoil *my* home, *my* life, then no one has to ask. I volunteer, because it *is* my home. You're just a tourist passing through. If you're not careful, you may break things you can never fix."

"Which is my advantage," Bolan countered. "If you buy in, when the smoke clears, you still have to live here."

"Not a problem, brother, if we do it right the first time."

"A hundred to one, and you still want a piece of it?" Bolan inquired.

"Ninety-three against two if your math's right," Johnson said.

"Make that ninety-three against three," Aolani said, cutting in.

"Hold on, now."

She flared at him instantly. "Don't even start with me, Ron. That macho shit won't fly. I'm in on this from the beginning, hear me?"

"Leia, if we're talking about fighting, now—"

"Then I've already seen it and survived it," Aolani interrupted.

"Just a taste, so far," Johnson replied.

"Serve up the rest. I'll handle it."

Bolan stayed in his neutral corner while they argued, but he quickly saw that Aolani wasn't backing down. Johnson appeared to get it, too, after a few more heated rounds.

"I'll miss you, girl," he said at last, "if something happens to you over this."

"Well, I'm a big girl."

"I know," Johnson said, and winked. "We all agreed, then?"

Bolan nodded, leaving his face in neutral.

"Right then. *Hele* on, big girl and boys," Johnson said, grinning hugely. "Let's go see some toys."

North Shore, Oahu

JOHNSON LIVED midway between Waimea Bay and Waialee, the next town to the north along Kamehameha Highway. His home had started out as a dilapidated bungalow and grown from there, with no coherent style, until it took on a distinctive character. The pink paint on its stucco walls had faded to the point that it was barely recognizable. Plastic flamingos in the scruffy yard added a nice note of self-mockery that fit with Johnson's character.

Inside, the place was decorated for a bachelor's comfort. Aolani found it homey, but she missed the softer touches of her own apartment, wondering if she could ever go back there again. Was it staked out by killers? Had they gone inside and trashed the place already, trying to discover where she'd gone with Polunu and Cooper?

"Anybody want a beer?" their host asked.

"Not while I'm working," Bolan said.

"Hey, that's the best time," Johnson countered. "But, to each his own."

"I'm still not clear about your background," Bolan said.

"A lot like yours, I'm guessing," Johnson said. "I did some time in uniform, then segued into other things. My Uncle Sam kept telling me they were legit. It didn't always feel that way."

"So, you retired?"

"After the third or fourth time that it nearly killed me. Sure, why not? Whatever I owed Uncle, it was paid off long ago."

"But now, you want back in?"

"A pickup game, that's all," Johnson replied. "For hearth and home, not God and country."

"You said something about toys?"

"Downstairs."

They followed Johnson to the kitchen, where an open pantry

door revealed, not shelves and foodstuffs, but a staircase slanting steeply into darkness. Johnson hit a wall switch, and the shadows vanished in a white fluorescent glare.

He led the way downstairs, with Aolani following, then Polunu and Bolan bringing up the rear. Aolani gasped when she saw Johnson's basement.

It was smallish, on the claustrophobic side, and sudden death from wall to wall.

How many guns? She gave up counting at two dozen, without getting to the pistols, hung with steel pegs through their trigger guards. The standing racks held rifles, shotguns, other weapons that she didn't recognize by name. Against the far wall, rocket launchers lined up in a tidy row, bulky projectiles sprouting from their muzzles like okra pods cast out of steel. Atop a central table, she saw cases of grenades and ammunition, all with military markings.

"Jesus, Ron!"

"Judge not, big girl," he answered, smiling wistfully. "We all need hobbies."

"You expecting Armageddon?" Bolan asked.

"I wasn't," Johnson answered. "But you seem to think it might be coming."

"That's the question."

"And to get the answer, you need someone in the know. Correct? But anyone like that will have his guard up now, big-time. You can't just wander up and ask, okay? You have to deal with them from strength."

"I'd rather not blow up the island," Bolan said, to Aolani's great relief.

"But maybe shake it up a little, eh? That's not always a bad thing."

"No."

"So, you've got tools already, have you?" Johnson asked.

"I liberated some."

"The price is right. You have full-auto capability?"

"An AK, but I'm short on magazines and ammunition."

"Then, you've come to the right place," Johnson replied.

Aolani stepped forward. "Listen, since we're doing this," she told the two men, "I should have a gun, myself."

Bolan asked her, "Have you ever fired one?"

"No," she said, defiantly. "But how hard can it be?"

"Firing is easy," Johnson said. "Hitting real live people when it matters, not so much."

"I'll manage, if I have to," Aolani told him.

"But you don't have to," Bolan said. "That's the point."

"In case you missed it," she replied, "those psychos at the Punchbowl tried to kill me, too. And Polunu."

Johnson turned to eye Polunu. "How about you? Want a gun?"

"Not me," Polunu replied. "I gave it up for Lent."

"That's funny," Johnson told him. "You're a funny guy."

And then, to Aolani, "So, you've never handled iron before. We'll keep it light and easy."

He went browsing through the pistols and came back to Aolani with a small black pistol. Cupped in her palm, it weighed roughly one-and-a-quarter pounds.

"The Walther PPK," Johnson said. "James Bond's gun. If you like the feel of it, we'll load her up and you'll be good to go."

Aolani raised the gun, aimed at a point on the wall.

"Two hands is better for stability," Johnson suggested. "You've got double action there, meaning that once it's loaded, with a live round in the chamber, all you have to do is pull the trigger. No need to be messing with the hammer."

"Good," she told both men, and squeezed the trigger once, dry-firing for the feel of it. "Let's load it, then."

"OKAY," JOHNSON SAID when they'd finished going through his arsenal. "We need to shake some cages, right?"

"Shake loose some information," Bolan said. "I'm not just in it for the agitation, with the numbers running."

"Right," Johnson replied. "Fact is, I've had my eye on Pele's

Fire for the past year or so. Nothing intrusive, but it doesn't need to be. You want to know something, the streets will fill you in, sooner or later."

"Later may be too late, this time," Bolan told him.

"Roger that. But I can tell you what they're into—some of it, at least—and show you where they make their money."

"Cash comes from donations," Polunu said. Despite his traitor's status, he still seemed concerned about the movement's reputation.

"Correction," Johnson said. "*Some* of the cash comes from donations. The rest, in case you didn't know, comes from a lot of shady deals."

"What do you mean?" Aolani asked.

"Name it," Johnson said. "Drug-dealing covers most of it, though."

"That's not true!" Polunu blurted, angry color rising in his face.

"Someone forgot to tell you, brother?" Johnson grinned. "Well, never mind. The CIA's been doing it for fifty years or more. What's good enough for Uncle Sam…"

"I don't believe you," Polunu answered stubbornly.

"That's your prerogative. Meanwhile, I know a couple of the importers who're dealing with the group. By reputation, anyway. Their go-between on dope deals is a guy called Happy Kiemela, operating out of Haleiwa, down the coast a bit."

"That can't be right," Polunu said. "I know this man."

"You mean your people kept you in the dark on something else?" Johnson replied. "There's a surprise."

"You think he'd know something about our problem?" Aolani asked.

"You mean, 'Surf's up. Fire from the sea.'?" Johnson shrugged. "I can't promise anything, but he may know where the money's going. If he doesn't, maybe he can buck us further up the food chain."

"Great," Aolani replied. "When do we go?"

"*We* don't," Bolan informed her, bracing for the angry

outburst that was sure to follow. "You'll be watching Polunu while we have a little talk with Happy."

"That's what *you* think," Aolani said.

"Listen," he told her sternly. "Just because you've heard some bullets whistle past your head doesn't make you combat trained or ready. If you're hunting payback, do it on your own time. This is too important."

"I'm not hunting anything," Aolani replied. "I want to help. I need to help. Oahu is my home, not yours."

"All the more reason not to slow us down, babe," Johnson said.

"Don't 'babe' me, damn it! I can pull my own weight." She turned on Bolan. "You! You wouldn't even know this guy, if not for me. I'm not the babysitter."

"It's the same job you were doing when I got here," he reminded her. "What's different, now?"

"I'm different, okay? They tried to kill me!"

"And they failed. There's no reason to let them have a second chance, especially when it could jeopardize the mission."

"That's it, then, I suppose? The men have spoken?"

"Pretty much."

"And where am I supposed to do this babysitting?" she demanded.

"Why not here?" Johnson asked. "Lanakila's people can't connect us. You'll be safer here than any place you're known to frequent."

"Just wait here, while you're off playing soldier?"

"No one's playing," Bolan told her. "Try to get that through your head. It's do-or-die. Maybe it's do-*and*-die, for all I know. The job I need for you to do, right now, is take care of him. That's it."

"Right. I guess I've got no choice," Aolani replied.

"You always have a choice," Bolan said. "Knowing how to make the right one is the rub."

"All right, then. You want me to hold the fort, that's what I'll do. One thing to think about before you go, though."

"What's that?" Johnson asked.

"How long are we supposed to wait?" She raised a questioning eyebrow. "I mean, what happens if you don't come back?"

Johnson responded with a shrug. "I own the place. The bills are paid up for the month. Stay put, or reach out to somebody you can trust. If we don't make it back, you're on your own."

"You talked to someone earlier," Bolan said, "or I wouldn't be here. Use the links you have, and keep your head down."

"Right. Okay."

"We ready?" Johnson asked.

"We're ready," Bolan said.

7

North Shore, Oahu

Joey Lanakila paced the room before two dozen of his best and brightest men, watching as their eyes followed his every move. Eddie Nahoa stood off to one side, silent, as if hoping the others wouldn't notice he was there. His eyes darted incessantly from Lanakila to the seated men of Pele's Fire, then back again.

Like he was watching tennis, Lanakila thought.

He might've smiled at that, if not for the volcanic pit of acid churning in his stomach and the headache throbbing like a bass drum on the nerves behind his eyeballs.

His audience was primed. They knew there had been bloody trouble overnight, that some of their good friends were dead, or missing and presumed dead. All knew that the day of *haole* reckoning was fast approaching, though they had not been entrusted with the details, for the sake of absolute security.

"Okay, we're all here now," Lanakila said. "It's an early day for some of you, but suck it up. We're in the middle of a four-alarm emergency, and this is not a drill."

It pleased him to echo the words broadcast over Pearl Harbor on that Sunday morning, more than half a century ago. The warning had been too late for the *haoles* then, and it would be too late when Lanakila unleashed hell upon them in the new millennium.

"In case some of you haven't heard the latest news, we're down seven men in the past ten hours. Tommy Puanani's crew got hit at the Punchbowl, wiped out. Then someone snatched Bobby Niele from his place in Waikiki and blew his brains out, left him on an island in Honolulu Harbor. Common sense says it must be the same person or group responsible for all of it."

His audience began to mutter, whispering among themselves.

"I know what some of you are thinking," Lanakila said. "You're wondering if one or two men could take Tommy's six-man team. I've got no answer for you. Honestly, we don't know who in hell's responsible, but someone did it. Someone owes us big-time, and we're going to collect."

The noise that went around the room this time was more approving, like the rumble of a lynch mob.

"Now, since we don't know who pulled the triggers," he pressed on, "our only way to solve this is to push ahead with what Tommy was doing when we lost it. If he touched a nerve somewhere, we're going to hit the same nerve, and keep hitting it until somebody screams. As soon as someone hostile shows his face, we bury him. For Tommy, Bobby and the rest."

"It wasn't pigs?" somebody asked from the back row.

"That's negative," Lanakila said. "If you've watched the TV news at all, you've seen them scurrying around, scratching their heads and talking shit about 'important leads.' That means they don't know anything. If pigs did this, they'd call it self-defense and brag about it in the headlines. This was someone else."

That shut them up while Lanakila paced in front of them for several silent seconds.

"How many of you know Mano Polunu?" he demanded.

They were muttering again, but cautiously, glances shooting back and forth around the audience before a cautious show of hands. Approximately half the audience dared to admit acquaintance with a traitor.

"Then you know," Lanakila continued, "that he lost his balls and quit the movement five, six weeks ago. Made noise as he was leaving that suggested he might spill some of our secrets to the pigs. Tommy's team was looking for Polunu last night, when they bought it. Polunu was supposed to hook up with a so-called home-rule activist named Leia Aolani. Anybody know her?"

No hands, this time. Several shaking heads.

"Maybe you saw her in the papers and forgot," he said. "She's one of those respectable Hawaiian nationalists who wouldn't raise a hand against a *haole* if she caught them gangbanging her mama."

Sparse, strained laughter.

"Anyway," Lanakila said, "Tommy and his boys went to collect those two and never made it home. And now, Niele's in a body bag. The only way to stop this shit and keep our plans on schedule is to find Polunu and his bitch. I want them both picked up and brought to me before the day's out. Someone on this island knows where we can find them. Find that someone, squeeze him shitless till he talks, and bring him here to me! Questions?"

A lone hand levitated from the middle of the audience.

"Let's hear it."

George Inaki asked, "Is someone sitting on their places, watching? I mean, just in case?"

"Good question. If they aren't, somebody should be. Take a couple boys and check it out, why don't you? Eddie can supply their home addresses. Any other questions?"

There were none. Lanakila swept his eyes across the upturned faces. Some of them looked eager, others apprehensive. He related to both moods.

"All right," he said, "we're done here. Hit the streets and don't come back until the job's done. Mano Polunu and his bitch. Alive, if possible, but bring them in!"

Haleiwa, Oahu

THE DEALER'S HOUSE wasn't a beachfront property, likely because its occupant demanded privacy. Hawaiian law guaranteed public access to all beaches and shorelines, including those encompassed by the grounds of private homes or posh estates.

No private beach existed in the Aloha State, a circumstance that drove some hermit-types inland.

Happy Kiemela didn't qualify for hermit status, but he didn't advertise his presence on the North Shore, either. With one foot in each of two supposedly conflicting worlds—the drug trade, and the revolutionary work of Pele's Fire—he walked a tightrope that could snap at any second, spilling him into a prison cell or open grave. It was especially important for Lanakila's movement that the group not be connected with drug trafficking or any other type of so-called "*haole* crime."

Too bad, Bolan thought, as he parked a block away from the Kiemela homestead and prepared to give the dealer's tightrope a dramatic shake.

Or maybe slash it out from under him completely.

"Not much to the house," Bolan observed, "unless he's gone hog-wild out back."

"Not Happy," Johnson replied. "He's got the revolution in his heart, brother. Drug-dealing is only a means to an end."

Bolan made no attempt to mask his skepticism. "So he says."

A shrug from Johnson. "Does he skim some of the profits for himself? It wouldn't stun me. But I doubt he's sitting on a fortune."

"Doesn't matter, either way," Bolan said. "All I want from Happy is information about Pele's Fire."

"You never mentioned who you work for," Johnson said.

"Neither did you."

"Touché. You ever feel like stepping back and standing down?"

"It's crossed my mind," Bolan allowed.

"But…?"

"But my work's not finished yet."

"You have a deadline?" Johnson asked him, smiling.

"When I work myself out of a job, I'll know it," Bolan said.

"Good luck with that. I gave the government too many years. There was a while when I thought they were the best years of my life. Lucky for me, it turned out I was wrong."

"You're happy, then?"

"Damn right."

"So, why this interruption?" Bolan asked.

"I told you at the house, these punks are messing with my home, my paradise." The grin came back. "Besides, I get the itch sometimes."

"Ready to scratch it, then?"

The surfer nodded. "Ready as I'll ever be."

They'd driven once around the block, scanning the target and its various approaches. Bolan had seen nothing to suggest an ambush, no sentries positioned on the street, but he could not see into Happy Kiemela's house or fenced backyard. For all they knew, the dealer could have fifty shooters tucked away and waiting for the first hint of a threat.

Or not.

"Any idea why he's called Happy?" Bolan asked his blond companion.

"Sorry. Not a clue."

One change of disposition, coming up, Bolan thought.

It was a fair walk from the rented car to Kiemela's driveway, with no cover in between. They had decided to be church folk, since the standard door-to-door evangelists wore plain suits even at the height of summer, sweating gallons as they covered endless miles, spreading the Word.

Bolan wore the Beretta 93-R underneath the wrinkled jacket from his carry-on, with the appropriated Glock tucked in his waistband at the back. The folding-stock Kalashnikov was jammed into his left armpit and clamped against his rib cage like a rigid spinal brace. A cautious eye might spot the bulge of its curved magazine, but by the time Bolan got that close to his target, there'd be no significant reaction time remaining.

Johnson had an Uzi submachine gun slung beneath his right arm, hanging muzzle-down under his neatly pressed black jacket. On the left, he had a SIG-Sauer P-226 tucked in his waistband, with the butt turned forward for a cross-hand draw.

His pockets sagged with extra magazines, the Bible in his left hand a distraction for unwary eyes.

"You feel the spirit, Brother Cooper?" he inquired, as they drew closer to their target.

"I feel something," Bolan granted, "but I don't think it's the Holy Ghost."

"Maybe we'll find some other ghosts," Johnson replied. "Or make some. Either way."

He sounded casual about it, as if killing wouldn't faze him. Bolan focused on the house, watching for flickers at the windows, anything to tell him they were being watched.

No movement yet. But if and when it came, the first glimpse Bolan had might be his last.

Turning onto the walkway that would lead them to the dealer's door, he plastered on a smile and said, "I wouldn't be surprised."

North Shore, Oahu

"Listen," Polunu said, "I'm not so sure we ought to do this."

"Fine," Aolani replied, without a backward glance. "You stay here, then. Do whatever the hell they tell you to. I need to check my place and see if anyone's been looking for me. My cats may need food, and I've got things I can't afford to lose, you understand?"

"Is your life one of them?"

She rounded on him then, her cheeks flaming, mad enough to spit. "Polunu, nobody's asking you to come with me. Stay here, where it's safe, and I'll come back after I've had a look around my place. Four hours for the round-trip, plus a little time to look inside. How's that?"

"Great, unless someone grabs you at the house or blows your brains out," Polunu said.

He had a point, of course, but she was too angry to back down now. Besides, she had the James Bond pistol in her handbag, fully loaded now.

"I'm going—deal with it."

Polunu looked as if he might burst into tears, but then the weepy moment passed, and he replied, "Okay, I'm going with you, then."

She almost told him to forget about it, nearly ordered him to stay at Johnson's house where he was safe and could report where she had gone, in case something went wrong.

Almost.

"Come on, then," she replied instead. "Do you have everything you need?"

"I'd like a Kevlar suit and one of those invisibility devices if your boyfriend's got one in his basement," Polunu said.

"He's not my boyfriend."

Aolani turned her back on Polunu and proceeded toward the door.

"I'm going," she informed him. "If you plan on coming with me, hurry up!"

Polunu fell in behind her, looking sheepish and abused, as if he were a child who'd just been scolded by his angry mother. Aolani didn't try to soothe his ruffled feelings, pausing only long enough to lock the door to Johnson's house behind her as they left.

Johnson had left his own car key with Aolani, as he'd said, in the event of an emergency. It fit an old Jeep sitting in the graveled driveway. As she climbed into the driver's seat, Aolani was thankful she knew how to drive a stick shift.

She revved the Jeep's engine, backed cautiously out of the driveway with gravel crunching underneath the vehicle's fat tires and headed southward on Kamehameha Highway. Aolani was reversing the course they had followed to reach Johnson's home from Honolulu, hoping that two hours and change would put her in her own familiar neighborhood.

What happened after that, she guessed was up to Fate or one of the Hawaiian gods some of her people still worshipped in a halfhearted way.

Aolani didn't plan to stay at home. She told herself that she would return to Johnson's house, to find out how he'd done with Cooper in their search for vital information. At the moment, though, she felt both angry and ignored, left out of what she'd hoped would be a shared event.

What are you thinking? asked a small voice in her head. Why would you even want to be a part of what they're doing now?

In truth, she didn't want to be a part of it—the fighting, killing, ducking bullets—but she would have liked the option to decline. She hated being pushed aside because she was a woman, or a Polynesian woman, or just too damned weak to pull her own weight in some man's eyes.

"We're going back after, right?" Polunu asked, as if he could read her mind.

"Of course we're going back. I'm not a car thief. I'll have a look around my place, that's all. Make sure nothing's wrong, and that my cats have enough food and water, and then we're out."

"I hope so," Polunu said. "I really hope so."

"Have some faith," Aolani said. "Have I ever steered you wrong?"

Haleiwa, Oahu

NO ONE ANSWERED the second ring of Happy Kiemela's doorbell, or the third. Bolan stepped backward from the door, casually examining the windows visible from where he stood on Kiemela's porch, but all were masked by heavy drapes.

"This sucks," Johnson said.

Bolan had planned for all eventualities, from semicordial greetings to a burst of gunfire as they crossed the dealer's lawn, but he had not considered standing on the doorstep of an empty house.

"You want to look around out back?" Johnson asked.

"Might as well."

Bolan glanced up and down the quiet street. No sign of neighbors watching, but it wouldn't have to be that obvious. An eyeball peering through a gap in curtains or venetian blinds, a call to 911, and prowl cars rolling silently while Bolan and his sidekick trespassed on expensive private property. With guns, no less.

And yet, they'd come this far. It seemed silly to turn around and leave, without at least a glimpse into the backyard.

They left the porch and moved around to the north side of the house, where a tall wrought-iron gate blocked entry to a fenced backyard. Bolan checked the latch and was surprised to find no lock in place, likewise no warning posted that the owner's dogs would cheerfully devour any trespassers.

He shook the gate lightly, a gentle rattling sound, then whistled softly, just in case a guard dog was asleep on duty.

Nothing.

"After you," Johnson said, with another crooked grin.

Bolan pushed through the gate, one hand on the Beretta in its quick-draw holster now. He wished that he had taken time to screw on the suppressor, but it wouldn't fit the holster then, and he had opted for a normal look, without clumsy sacks of weapons.

Twice they passed windows, ducking below what had to be the kitchen's, with its lacy curtains, walking upright past another shrouded by beige drapes. The strip of grass they followed lay in shade, so Bolan had no fear of casting shadows on the curtains.

Kiemela's backyard wasn't huge, but it was well designed and lovingly maintained. There was an oval swimming pool, some decking with tasteful patio furniture, and an elaborate-looking stainless-steel barbecue with a propane tank underneath it. Near the pool, a naked man sprawled on a cedar chaise lounge, his face toward the sky.

Bolan and Johnson moved to flank him. As they neared the chaise lounge, Bolan realized the stranger wore some kind of G-string swimsuit smaller than a standard jock strap. All the rest of him was dusky bronze—part of it natural, according to his Polynesian features, while the hue was augmented by long exposure to the sun.

Bolan glanced back in the direction of the house, but

glimpsed no movement on the far side of glass sliding doors. If there were guards inside, he'd have to take them as they came.

The man stirred as their shadows fell across him, one from either side. He blinked up at them, dropped a hand to snare a pair of sunglasses that lay beside his chair and slipped them on.

"You're in the wrong place, bruddahs," he informed them.

"Not if this is Happy Kiemela's house," Bolan replied.

The bare hint of a smile vanished. "Who wants to know?"

"We'll ask the questions," Bolan said. "Are you—"

"It's him," Johnson interrupted. "In the flesh, unfortunately."

"Hey, you don't like what you see, get off my fucking property. In fact, get off whether you like or not."

"We won't take too much of your time," Bolan replied. "A few quick questions."

"So, you're cops? Is that it? Jesus, I thought even *haole* cops had better suits than those. Listen, we've done this dance. I'm tired of it. You want to cuff me, take me in, go for it. My first call triggers the lawsuit for harassment that my lawyer warned your chief about last time. It's not a great career move, but I leave it up to you. Fuck off, or put the bracelets on and fuck yourselves."

"I'm sure that speech would be impressive," Johnson said, "if we were the police."

"Well, shit, who are you? Feds? Did D.C. scrap its dress code?"

Bolan produced the sweaty AK-47. Johnson showed his Uzi. Both muzzles were angled down toward Kiemela's startled face.

"We're not the welcoming committee, Happy," Bolan said.

"No, wait!" His hands rose futilely, as if mere flesh and blood could block twin streams of military spec bullets. "I can double what you're being paid for this, I promise you!"

"We're not mercs, brother," Johnson told him. "This is a labor of love."

"Well, Christ, there must be something! Tell me what you want. Just name it!"

"Pele's Fire," Bolan said.

"Okay. What about it?"

"They've got a big luau coming up, sometime within the next few days," Johnson explained. "We need to know what *you* know, about what they're doing, where it's happening, and when."

"Oh, Jesus, man. You think they tell *me* shit like that? I'm just an earner, get it? I put money in their pockets, plenty of it, but they don't brief me on strategy. Try something else. *Anything* else!"

"You don't know anything about six missing sailors?" Bolan asked.

"Just what I've seen on the tube. People disappear every day, man. You saying the Fire did that thing?"

Bolan glanced up at Johnson, got a frown back in return.

"So, let me get this straight," Bolan said. "You sell dope for terrorists and pass the money on to them, but they don't keep you in the loop on what they're doing otherwise?"

"That's it! You got it, man, I swear!"

"I guess you're useless, then," Bolan replied, and swung the butt of his Kalashnikov down into Happy Kiemela's face.

Honolulu

"THAT PLACE of Polunu's was a flea trap," Lawrence Kilenowuka said.

"You mean a fire trap," Tom Palanaka said, correcting him.

"Don't tell me what I mean. I said a *flea* trap."

"Well, we shoulda burned it, anyway," Palanaka replied. "Kill fleas and teach the rat a lesson, all at once."

"Polunu's not going back there," George Inaki said. "Bastard's a traitor, but that doesn't make him stupid."

"He'll feel pretty fucking stupid when we nail him," Palanaka said.

"You think Tommy Puanani said the same thing on his way out to the Punchbowl?" Inaki asked.

No response to that from either of his men, which was good. Inaki wanted them to use their heads, instead of talking shit about how bad they were until it got them killed, and maybe him along with them.

They were rolling north on Dillingham Boulevard, toward Leia Aolani's place on Colburn Street. She had a small house, mortgaged to the hilt, and while Inaki knew it had been checked before, not once but several times, he hoped their luck might change.

In any case, Lanakila had commanded that they go back through the loop, on the off chance that Polunu or the woman might go home. Or, maybe, that the first teams sent to check out their places had missed something, let something fall through the cracks.

It would be bad for whoever had done the first sweep, if Inaki's crew found anything useful. He thought about that for a moment, then told himself screw 'em.

More than likely, Tommy Puanani and his boys had done the first sweep after Polunu had split from Pele's Fire. In which case, Lanakila couldn't punish them beyond what they'd already suffered at some stranger's hands.

His master's words echoed inside Inaki's head, now.

Don't come back until the job's done. Polunu and his bitch. Alive, if possible, but bring them in!

Of course, the hitch to grabbing them was finding them. Inaki didn't know if they were still in Honolulu—or still in Hawaii, for that matter. If he couldn't find them, though, he knew his ass was in a bind.

Don't come back until the job's done.

Meaning never.

If Inaki knew that they would fail, the best thing he could do was drop the others off somewhere and drive like hell away from Honolulu. Maybe up into the mountains, if he couldn't catch a flight for Indonesia, Singapore, New Zealand.

Any fucking place but here.

He turned left on Kalihi Street, then right on Colburn, slowing as he started reading the addresses. "Call out if you see it," he commanded. "That's 4418."

"Evens are on the right," Kilenowuka said.

"Okay. Good."

"There it is—4416," Palanaka announced.

And there it was. Not much to look at, but a tidy place, a little on the small side, but well kept. Inaki wondered whether it was trashed inside, or if the other teams had simply waited on the street to see who came and went.

"I need a place to park," he said, already scanning curbs.

"Up on your left," Kilenowuka said. "Right there."

"Wrong way. I'll have to come around the block."

Inaki gave the Ford more gas, anxious to be on station now and do his job. Whatever Tommy Puanani and the rest had done before him, Inaki wasn't waiting on the street and wasting countless hours in the hope that Aolani or Polunu might appear. He meant to have a look inside, and maybe wait there for them.

Wait how long?

He'd have to think about that.

They'd been ordered not to come back empty-handed, but he couldn't sit forever in the woman's little house. The day of *haole* reckoning was fast approaching, and Inaki didn't plan to be one of the sluggish fools who hung around with his thumb up his ass, until it all went up in smoke.

Come home and see us, bitch. He beamed the thought through space toward Aolani, hoping she received it somehow, somewhere.

But if not, he had a deadline in his mind, beyond which he would cut and run.

8

Honolulu

Aolani had learned something from Matt Cooper. As she turned Johnson's Jeep into the southern end of Colburn Street, she scanned both sides for strangers, anything that struck her as being out of place.

A hint of danger waiting to engulf her.

Aolani didn't know her neighbors well. It was the curse of living in a modern city, leading an active life. When not at work or busy with political concerns, she liked her privacy and did not mingle with the strangers who surrounded her. She knew a few of them by name, but paid no real attention to their cars, their movements, or their visitors.

Which was a problem now that she was being hunted like an animal and every vehicle seemed ominous, each glance from someone who she didn't recognize seemed a potential threat.

But it was quiet on her street this morning, no two ways about it. Most of Aolani's neighbors would be off to work by now, the homemakers among them busy running errands to the supermarket, dry cleaners, whatever people did when they had time to spare and terrorists weren't breathing down their necks with murderous intent.

She passed the house, surveyed it with a wary eye, and found she could see nothing out of place. Did that mean she was safe?

"I don't see anything," Polunu said, once again displaying his apparent skill at mind reading.

"I'll go once more around the block," she told him. "To be sure."

"Okay," he answered, slumping lower in his seat.

The open Jeep made Aolani feel exposed. She missed her Datsun Maxima and wondered if the cops had traced it to her yet. Had they come calling at the house in uniform, giving her neighbors cause to gossip?

There was no yellow crime scene tape around her house, no business cards or notes tacked to her door, as far as she could see. Did that mean the police had not been there, or were they waiting for a warrant from a sluggish judge?

If they *were* waiting, would they leave someone to watch the place? And if so, why were there no police cars in evidence?

Next time around the block, she slowed on the approach to number 4416, the place she had called home for nearly four years, now. She swung the Jeep into the driveway, hesitated for another beat, then switched off the engine.

"You want to wait out here?" she asked Polunu.

"You kidding me? I'll be a goddamned sitting duck."

"If there was anybody here, we'd both be dead by now," she said.

"Just 'cause they aren't sitting in your driveway," he replied, "doesn't mean they won't drive by within the next five minutes."

Aolani knew he had a point. Whatever she was doing at the house, whatever had compelled her to return here in the midst of what amounted to a private war, she should be quick about it. In and out, with no unnecessary foot-dragging. Top up the cat's food and water. Grab whatever odds and ends she could remember, for her comfort on the run, without collecting so much that it slowed her.

She placed her handbag on her lap and opened it, reached in, half drew Johnson's Walther pistol. It felt heavier than when he had placed it in her hands, as if the possibility of using it against another human being had increased the compact weapon's weight.

"Aolani," her tense companion hissed at her, "don't flash that thing out here, okay?"

"Just checking," she assured him.

Aolani pulled out the Jeep's ignition key and put it in her bag, then rummaged deeper for her own key ring. She found it, gripped the front door's key in her left hand, then slung the purse over her shoulder, so that she could keep her right hand buried in it, on the pistol, for their short walk to the house.

"Ready or not," she said to Polunu, "here we go."

Her feet felt heavy, almost leaden, as she moved around the Jeep and followed the familiar concrete path to her front door. White-knuckling the Walther, Aolani tried the doorknob first and was relieved to find it locked, as she had left it.

She used the key next, stepped into her living room with Polunu on her heels. She'd been gone less than a day, yet she thought that it had acquired a musty smell. Or was that—

"Welcome home," a male voice said from close behind her as the door swung shut.

Aolani half turned to find a stranger in the corner she had failed to check, aiming a pistol at the back of Polunu's head.

"And Mano Polunu, too," another voice declared, this one from the direction of her kitchen, where she saw two more strangers with guns.

The second man who'd spoken smiled at Aolani and remarked, "Looks like our lucky day."

North Shore, Oahu

"I REALLY THOUGHT he'd know something," Johnson said, as they left Happy Kiemala's house behind.

"Not your fault," Bolan told him, "but we're still right where we started."

Meaning that he didn't have a clue to Lanakila's plans for what he called the main event.

Surf's up! Fire from the sea!

So, what the hell?

"I guess Happy was just the earner," Johnson said. "Maybe I should've figured that, instead of wasting time on him."

Bolan never considered taking out a major drug smuggler a waste of time, but he still felt the sense of urgency that Johnson seemed to share. There had been something about Happy Kiemala's place….

"You knew him," Bolan said.

"I knew *of* him. As you saw, he didn't know my ass from Adam's."

"Still. You take away the politics, was he a standard-issue dealer?"

"How'd you mean?"

"He was alone this morning," Bolan said. "I've never known a dealer moving any kind of weight who didn't have at least one bodyguard in residence."

Johnson considered that and nodded. "No, you're right. The times I've seen him on the town, he always had a couple of burly goons from Pele's Fire in tow. Some kind of status trip, I thought, or something to legitimize him. Give him credibility outside the trade."

"No guards today, unless they overslept."

"I should've caught that," Johnson said. "I'm not just rusty, man. I'm growing barnacles."

"What does the lack of muscle mean to us, if anything?" Bolan asked.

Johnson frowned. "Manpower shortage?" he suggested. "If they're seven down since you blew in last night, they may be feeling it."

"Enough to leave their major earner that exposed?"

"I wouldn't have expected it," Johnson admitted.

"No. Neither would I. Unless all hands were needed somewhere else, in preparation for—"

"The main event," Johnson completed Bolan's thought. "Whatever *that* may be."

"I've been attacking this from the wrong end," Bolan told his companion. "Lanakila's people threw my game off when I landed, with their first ambush. Since then, it's been a catch-up game, but I'm not catching up. My fault."

"You have a new play book somewhere?" Johnson inquired.

"I might."

Driving with one hand, Bolan palmed his sat phone, keyed the speed-dial for Hal Brognola's home and winced at the idea of waking him a second time.

When Brognola came on the line, sounding as alert as ever, Bolan said, "I need Joey Lanakila's phone numbers, starting with cell and any private lines, then working back from there until he's covered. Can do?"

"How soon do you need it?" Brognola asked.

"Yesterday."

"I'll buzz the Farm and call you back in ten, maybe fifteen."

"Talk then," Bolan said, cutting the connection.

"You have a fairy godmother?" Johnson asked.

"God*father*," Bolan replied. "He's good with data."

And a world of other useful things.

They were a block from Johnson's house when the surfer said, "Shit! My Jeep's gone."

Bolan eyed the empty gravel driveway. "Leia," he suggested.

"I left her the keys in case of an emergency," Johnson replied. "I never thought she'd use them, but she was pissed off about not going with us on the Happy run."

"She wouldn't have enjoyed it," Bolan said, swinging the rental car into the driveway.

"Maybe it's something simple," Johnson offered. "Like a female hygiene run."

"Maybe."

But Bolan didn't think so. Johnson's cautious movements as he stepped out of the car indicated that he really didn't think so, either.

"If she left her sidekick here, it should be cool," Johnson remarked.

"And if she didn't?"

"Then, we think of something else. She's old enough to make her own decisions. And, apparently, to steal my goddamned Jeep."

Johnson approached his own front door with key outstretched in one hand, while the other wrapped around his Uzi's pistol grip. Inside, they found the neat house quiet, cool and undisturbed.

"No struggle, anyway," Johnson said.

"Here, she left a note."

Bolan had spied it on the breakfast counter, a small piece of paper tented by folding it in two. The note read, simply: Gone to check my house. Back soon.

"Okay, she's burning off some steam," Johnson said. "But I guess it could be worse."

"Unless her house is covered."

"Right."

Unless she was already dead and gone.

Mililani Town, Oahu

"SHE'S A HOT ONE," George Inaki said. "I wouldn't mind taking a poke at her, myself."

"You brought her in," Eddie Nahoa said. "That's all I need from you, right now."

"Sure, I'm just saying—"

"See your group leader for reassignment. We won't have a minute free for partying until we're downwind from the main event."

"Yes, sir."

Inaki left, looking disgruntled, but Nahoa didn't give a damn about his feelings. Inaki could screw whoever he wanted on his own time, but Nahoa was not about to let a randy buck screw up the main event.

Before that happened, he would personally give Inaki two 9 mm pills to cure his problem, once and for all.

Nahoa had instructed Inaki's snatch team to meet him in Mililani Town, near the geographical heart of Oahu, for multiple reasons. First, it saved them the longer drive back to the North Shore with hostages. Second, it kept the two prisoners clear of Joey Lanakila's headquarters in hiding.

And third, it gave him time to work on them alone.

Lanakila, of course, had signed off on the plan, accepting Nahoa's argument about security. Lanakila had enough to think about right now, without further distractions, and Nahoa would of course provide a full report on anything he learned from Polunu or the woman.

Well, a nearly full report.

Since he'd received the word of Happy Kiemala's death due to a blow to the head, at home in Haleiwa, Nahoa had been seething to find out why Happy was selected. More importantly, he had to know if those responsible knew Kiemela had been supplying cocaine to him for the past twelve months or so. That kind of information in the wrong hands was enough to get him busted.

Hell, if Lanakila knew about his drug habit, it was enough to get him killed.

Nahoa didn't know if Polunu or the woman were involved somehow in Happy's sad demise, but he meant to find out if they were. He might ask that first thing, even before he started grilling them about the Punchbowl killings, Bobby Niele's death, or whatever it was they'd told the pigs.

Nahoa had dozens of questions roiling in his mind, but those related to his own survival obviously took priority.

Interrogation Central was a smallish house whose basement had been thoroughly soundproofed. They had tested it with fireworks, first, then gunfire. When the neighbors didn't bitch to the police, it had become the place where Lanakila and his minions dealt with traitors to the cause.

That didn't happen often—only twice before today, in fact—but those were memorable times. The thickly insulated walls absorbed the loudest screams without an echo, much less any leakage to the outside world. And they were draped with plastic tarps for easy cleanup, too.

Nahoa himself had hosed the blood out last time, watched it swirling down the twin drains planted in the concrete floor.

The basement had two drains because it had two chairs, both bolted to the floor. It made Nahoa think of signs he'd seen in barbershops, when he was just a kid: Two chairs, no waiting.

It was like that in the torture basement, too, except that one subject *would* have to wait while Nahoa operated on the other. That was fine, he thought, since the horrendous sights and screams, the grim anticipation of it all, would loosen up the second pigeon's tongue.

Access to the basement was achieved via a staircase hidden in a hallway closet. It required Nahoa to descend ten steps, then duck into a leftward-turning crouch before descending twelve more steps to solid ground. It would've been a painful ordeal in the dark, banging his head on beams above, but now the basement was awash with light below, guiding his steps.

And it was not Nahoa who would feel the pain to come.

The hostages were taped and handcuffed to their separate chairs. Both had been stripped in preparation for their questioning. The woman's breasts were blotched with livid marks, as if someone had pinched her. Still, her look was all defiance. Polunu's face, by contrast, was already streaked with tears.

Nahoa stood over the woman for a moment, then turned to her guard and asked, "Who touched her?"

"Sir?"

Nahoa felt the anger churning in his gut. "Who touched her, when my orders were that she *should not be touched?*"

He bellowed the last words into the sentry's face, bent close enough that spittle flecked the man's cheeks.

"Sir, I—I'm sorry, sir! I didn't think—"

Nahoa whipped a fist into the nervous guard's stomach, doubled him over with a retching sound from deep inside. His rising knee collided with the man's forehead, missed his nose deliberately to avoid bloodstains on trouser fabric, but the outcome was the same. The guard dropped on his back, writhing in pain.

Nahoa crouched beside him, close enough to whisper in his ear. "Next time you get the notion to ignore one of my orders, make damned sure you *do* think, first. Now drag your sorry ass upstairs, out of my sight."

Leaving the man to it, Nahoa turned and faced the woman, leaving Polunu out of it. "I'm sorry if you suffered some indignity from that *lolo*. In fact, I'm sorry we are here at all, but it comes down to this. You have to answer certain questions, and I can't stop asking till you do. You want to be a tough lady? Or you want to make it easy on yourself?"

Aolani said nothing.

Nahoa shrugged, said, "Okay, then," and crossed the basement to a corner where he found a rolling tray piled high with sharp steel implements. It jangled as he walked it back toward Aolani's chair.

"Your call, then, missy. We do this the hard way."

North Shore, Oahu

"YOU WOULDN'T KNOW her phone number, by any chance?"

"She's in the book," Johnson replied. "I looked her up a couple times, thought about calling her, but never got around to it."

"So, where's the book?"

"Phone nook, behind you."

Bolan found it, let his fingers do the walking until he found Aolani's listing, then used Johnson's telephone to dial her number. After it had rung two dozen times, he cradled the receiver.

"Either not there, or she isn't answering," he said.

"Could be the smart move, let it ring. Somebody checking on you doesn't know you're there."

"Could be."

But Bolan didn't think so.

He was reaching for the landline, ready for another futile effort, when his sat phone buzzed. Bolan saw Brognola's home number in the little LED window as he thumbed down the button to respond.

"What have you got?" he asked without preliminaries.

"Home and cell for now," Brognola said. "We're working on some other numbers for you."

"These may do it," Bolan said. "If they're no good, I'll ring you back."

"Okay. Ready?"

"Let's have them."

Brognola recited two phone numbers, one for Lanakila's home address, the second for his last-known cell phone. Bolan memorized them both, thanked Brognola and broke the link.

"Anything?" Johnson asked.

"Maybe something," Bolan answered.

He knew Lanakila wasn't at his former home address and hadn't been for weeks, at least. The address and the phone number that went with it were obsolete. Still, Bolan tried the number anyway, and hung up halfway through the typical recording telling him the number he had dialed was out of service.

That left one, assuming Lanakila hadn't ditched his last-known cell phone in favor of another—or a dozen others—since he vanished underground. It wasn't quite the long shot that his old home number had turned out to be, but it was close.

He made the call. Two rings before a cautious male voice answered at the other end.

"Yeah?"

"I need to speak with Joey Lanakila," Bolan said. Why stand on ceremony?

"Who is this?" the voice demanded.

"I'm the guy who smoked six of his men at the Punchbowl, and another on Sand Island."

"Hang on."

Three heartbeats passed, then the same voice returned. "I'm Lanakila. How'd you get this number?"

"Is that really what you want to ask me, Lanakila?"

"No, it isn't. Who are you, and why in hell are you doing this to me?"

"I thought you'd like some fireworks, Lanakila. Looking forward to the main event, and all."

More silence on the other end, before the boss of Pele's Fire replied, "You're bluffing, man. You don't know shit."

"I know you have two friends of mine on ice. Your life will take a turn from bad to worse, unless I get them back intact."

"What friends would those be, then?"

"Mano Polunu and the lady who was helping him."

Bolan refrained from giving Aolani's name, in case the enemy still didn't know it. Yet another long shot, but he liked to cover all his bases.

"Man, you're blowing smoke."

"Okay, then," Bolan said, "after I kill you, if I find out you were right, I'll tell your next of kin it was my bad."

"Kill *me?*" That brought a laugh from Lanakila, but it sounded forced to Bolan. Almost shaky. "You talk big, for somebody with no idea of where I am, or where his friends are."

"I'll find all of you before I'm done," Bolan assured him. "Anyway, the hunting's half the fun, right? By the time I'm done, you won't have any so-called soldiers left to help you with the main event. Or, should I make that sailors?"

He was bluffing, pulled the last jab out of nowhere, but it struck a nerve.

"Hold on, now, bruddah. I can always ask around, see maybe one of my guys met your friends and didn't think to fill me in about it, eh? Don't get all hasty, here."

"You've got ten minutes," Bolan said. "And any damage they may suffer in the meantime, you'll be getting back times ten."

"Where would I get in touch with you?" Lanakila asked.

"Right there, where you're standing," Bolan answered. "I'll call you."

Scowling, he cut the link.

LANAKILA IMMEDIATELY got Nahoa on his cell phone. Nahoa sounded tense, a little out of breath, then startled when he heard his master's voice.

"What's up?" Nahoa asked.

"You started on that project yet?" Lanakila asked.

"Just about to. Laying out the tools. You want to listen?"

"No, I want you to forget about it. Plans have changed."

"What do you mean, plans have changed?"

"Just what I said. You get 'em ready for the road, now, hear?"

"You talk stink, man! I don't know what the hell you're saying."

"Listen, Eddie, damn it! I just finished talking to the *haole* who did Tommy Puanani's team. He wants these two, big-time."

"Fuck what he wants, brah. You don't wanna kill him, let me do it."

"You forgetting who you're talking to, goddamn it?" Lanakila asked his oldest living friend. When he received no answer, he pushed on. "I'm *telling* you to get them ready now, and don't be messing with them while you do. Nothing. I want the bait for this big snapper nice and fresh."

"The bait?"

"Now, what you think? I'm gonna let him walk away from this?"

"I want to be there when he gets it," Nahoa said.

"That's what I had in mind, if you can do exactly what you're told."

"I'll do it, man. No sweat."

"Starting right now," Lanakila said, and he severed the connection.

His cell rang seconds later, taking Lanakila by surprise. It didn't seem as if he'd spent ten minutes talking to Nahoa, but their argument had eaten up his time. The cell phone's LED display revealed no number or address.

"Hello?"

"You get it set?" the grim voice asked.

"All set, man. Not to worry."

"I'm not worried," the stranger said. "If you blow it, you can worry out the time you've still got left."

"No need for threats, man. We collaborating here, or what?"

"Not even close."

"So, how are we supposed to help each other, then?"

"I'm giving you a chance to help yourself," the caller said. "By giving up my friends, unharmed, you buy yourself a little time."

Lanakila didn't like the sound of that, but since he wasn't playing by the nameless bastard's rules, it didn't weigh much on his mind.

"Okay, I hear you, man," he said. "So, what's the play?"

"I'll meet you at the Sacred Falls State Park. Know where it is?"

"Sure, I know where it is."

"I'll see you there at sundown."

"Man, do *you* know it's a forty-minute hike up to the falls, sometimes with mud knee-deep? It's not that easy in the daylight, man. At night, no lights, it can't be done."

"I said the park," his caller answered, "not the falls. Just bring my friends, unharmed. I'll take them off your hands."

"You know," Lanakila said, "Mano was a friend of mine before you ever knew him, and he's done me wrong. I owe him something, brah."

"You'll have to pay him later. Focus on priorities right now. You want the main event to fly, it'll cost you something."

"What's that little shit been telling you?"

"Nothing," the stranger answered. "That's the funny part, from my perspective. You've been losing all these men to bag a guy who couldn't hurt you, anyway."

"Says you."

"And I'm the only one you're talking to, so far."

Lanakila played a hunch. "You know, man, if you are some kind of Fed or something, this whole conversation's inadmissible."

"You teaching law now, Lanakila?"

"I'm just telling you what any pig should know, up front."

"Well, put your mind at ease," the caller said. "It never crossed my mind to file a charge on you. Three hours, at the park."

"Okay, just so—"

But he was talking to dead air. The caller had already cut him off.

Sundown. It could be worse. He had to rally every man he could lay hands on in a hurry, get them to the island's east coast, and be ready when the deadline rolled around.

Deadline.

He liked the sound of that.

Somebody would be dead when that time came, make no mistake.

9

Sacred Falls State Park, Oahu

Waiting for sundown was a gamble, but it had rewards. First up, there was no rush for Bolan and Johnson, following Oahu's coastline on Kamehameha Highway to their destination. They literally had all day to make a three-hour drive, which granted them time to choose weapons, feed themselves and relax after a fashion.

Second, while delaying the exchange might jeopardize the hostages, Bolan believed Lanakila was prepared to play the handoff by the rules—up to a point. If he intended to kill Aolani and Polunu, he could do it in five seconds. Adding hours to the mix might well increase their personal discomfort, but he reasoned that they would suffer no permanent damage.

Unless it was already done. In which case…

Bolan's third reason for stalling the exchange was that whenever possible, he liked to work in darkness. Johnson had suggested the exchange point and the hour, knowing they could be there well before their enemies.

And so they were.

The state park had been closed to tourists for years, but only warning signs prevented daredevils from marching through the darkness to their almost certain doom.

After securing their car well out of sight, they climbed a hundred feet or so to vantage points that overlooked the site's main parking lot. A lonely pole light did its best to keep the lot below them safe and visible to any passing sheriff's cars.

So far, they hadn't seen one, which was fine.

Bolan was carrying his AK, but he'd also borrowed one of Johnson's guns—specifically a Heckler & Koch PSG-1. The precision sniper rifle, with its six-power zoom telescopic sight and 20-round box magazine of 7.62 mm NATO rounds, would serve him well.

"They'll park somewhere down there," he told Johnson. "No choice. They may not like the light, but they'll be visible enough at this range."

"Head shots?" Johnson asked him.

"Shouldn't be a problem."

They had stopped off on the way and found a lonely dead-end road that led them off into the densely wooded mountains. At a roughly level spot with decent visibility, Bolan had sighted in the PSG-1, firing off a box of twenty rounds to test himself.

No sweat.

"I'll be a little closer," Johnson had decided, cradling a stubby Colt M-4 Commando carbine from his arsenal. It was a shorter version of the standard U.S. military's M-16 A-2, with all of the original's firepower, but you couldn't fault Johnson for wanting to be nearer to his targets, with that 11.5-inch barrel.

"Okay, then," Bolan answered. "All we have to do is settle down and wait."

"I'll see you after," Johnson told him.

"One way or another."

"You're catching on," the surfer said, and smiled.

Waiting was the hard part, if a hunter wasn't used to it. One of the first things any soldier learned was the old maxim, hurry up and wait. As far as Bolan could determine, that had been the unofficial motto of every military organization from biblical times to the twenty-first century. War itself was ninety percent waiting, and ten percent blind savagery.

This night, he only hoped that the wait was not too long.

There was an outside chance, he realized, that Lanakila might get tired of having hostages around and kill them for his

own amusement, maybe bring their corpses to the handoff as
a fuck-you gesture to his unknown enemy.

In which case, he would die.

Of course, Bolan already planned to kill whichever terrorists arrived with Aolani and Polunu. Bagging Lanakila would
be gravy, but he wasn't counting on it.

With that settled in his mind, Bolan began the breathing ex-
ercises that would help him to relax while staying perfectly
alert. Counting the minutes now, instead of hours.

Waiting for the savagery he knew so well.

"WE'RE ALMOST THERE," Jim Kima said, keeping both hands on
the steering wheel. "Two minutes, tops."

Eddie Nahoa, riding in the stolen Volvo's shotgun seat,
turned toward his three men in the rear and said, "Make double
sure you're cocked and locked."

He heard them racking slides and cocking levers in the
backseat, while he checked his own folding-stock AR-18
assault rifle. Nahoa had a 40-round box magazine locked into
the receiver, which he thought—no, make that hoped—would
be more ammo than he needed for this night's wet work.

But five more magazines were weighting down his pockets,
just in case.

He wondered if Leia Aolani could hear their guns, back in
the trunk. Nahoa hoped she was suffering in her confinement,
but he still felt cheated by having his session with Aolani cut
short before it had truly begun.

"Here we go," Kima said, interrupting his commander's
fantasy. He swung the Volvo off Kamehameha Highway into a
medium-sized parking lot.

"Stay away from that light," Nahoa said.

"No problem."

Behind them, Nahoa saw a second car turn in. It was a
Buick, also stolen, bearing five more of his men and Polunu in
its trunk. Nahoa had been tempted to tape over Polunu's mouth

and nostrils when they stashed him, let the little turncoat suffocate on their drive from the North Shore to the Sacred Falls State Park, but Lanakila had been quite emphatic about keeping them alive.

At least, until the trap was sprung.

It won't be long, he thought, and he had to wipe his sweaty palms, one at a time, along his trouser legs to improve his grip on the AR-18.

"This good enough?" Kima asked.

"Fine," Nahoa said.

The parking lot was small enough that they could not escape the light entirely, but at least their faces would be shadowed—until the muzzle-flashes from their weapons started lighting up the night.

The Buick parked beside them, leaving space for open doors, and soldiers started piling out. Nahoa walked back to the Volvo's trunk as Kima popped the lid, then raised it, peering down at Aolani nestled next to the spare tire.

He grabbed her roughly by one arm and dragged her halfway from the trunk. Nahoa hoped he bruised her in the process, but she made no sound, just scrambled clear as he released her, awkward with her wrists bound tightly behind her back.

"End of the road," Nahoa said. "Your *haole* knight in shining armor is supposed to be here, somewhere. So far, I don't see him."

"That's exactly when he nails you," Aolani answered.

"Sure he does. Let's go find out, shall we? See if he stood you up, or—"

Nahoa never had a chance to finish. He was steering Aolani with his left hand, clinging to his weapon with the right, when just in front of him Kima's head exploded.

Warm blood and brain matter spattered Nahoa's face, blinding him for a crucial instant as he flinched. He felt Aolani twist out of his grasp and start to run, then swung his rifle in her general direction, but refrained from firing out of fear that he might riddle his own men.

The echo of a rifle shot reached Nahoa, then, and he dropped to his knees, swiping the gore out of his eyes. He heard a second shot, and then a third, before his soldiers started firing back at someone, somewhere in the darkness.

Nahoa started firing, too, up toward the pitch-black hillside nearest to him, even though he couldn't see a thing to shoot at.

Go down fighting, said the small voice in his head. At least they can't say you were yellow at the end.

BOLAN'S FIRST SHOT took down the gunman standing in front of Aolani and slightly to her left. His target was the driver of the car who had disgorged her from its trunk a moment earlier. His bullet, traveling at half a mile per second, reached its mark before the echo of the shot could follow at the speed of sound, but the effects were instantly apparent and they galvanized the other shooters milling near the cars below.

Before he'd fired, Bolan had swept the faces visible and satisfied himself that Lanakila's wasn't one of them. He'd waited then, a few more heartbeats, until Aolani was revealed, extracted from the first car's trunk and planted on her feet. He didn't need to wait for Polunu, who had to logically be bundled in the second auto's trunk.

His PSG-1 didn't have a flash-hider attached, but Bolan's first shot had been unexpected, no one eyeballing the darkened slope in front of them as far as he could tell. His second shot came as they broke for cover, most of them feeling obliged to fire their weapons in his general direction, none of them so far presenting any concrete threat.

His second target would've been Nahoa, recognized from Brognola's files as the man who had pulled Aolani from the car's trunk, but the wiry terrorist had quick reflexes. First, he dropped into a crouch behind Aolani, then sprayed the night with automatic rifle fire and threw himself behind the car in which he had arrived.

Too late.

So, target number two became one of the flunkies, slower than the rest to find a hiding place. He was a big man, not too tall, but nearly square in build, the blunt stump of his head planted atop broad shoulders without any vestige of an intervening neck.

The target carried a submachine gun that looked like a toy in his hands, milking short bursts into the darkness before him. Bolan aimed for his center of mass and nailed him with a round through the chest. A tiny entrance wound in front, a gaping fist-sized exit pit behind.

The big man staggered, dropped his weapon, raising both hands to his punctured chest, then toppled slowly forward and collapsed facedown upon the asphalt.

Two for two.

By that time, Johnson had begun to rake the stragglers with his Colt M-4 Commando, firing short bursts like a pro. Bolan saw one man drop under the surfer's fire, before three others saw the autocarbine's muzzle-flash and poured return fire into Johnson's nest.

Had they been quick enough to nail him?

Bolan's first pang of concern evaporated when the carbine spoke again, this time from cover several yards beyond Johnson's first position. When the surfer fired again, another man went down, and the survivors made another dash for cover.

Four down, out of ten. The odds were getting better, but it all would be for nothing if Nahoa or one of his shooters killed the hostages.

Not necessarily, a voice in Bolan's head reminded him. Whoever dies tonight won't be participating in the main event—whatever that is.

Bolan didn't buy the dead-end logic. If he wiped out every soldier Lanakila had this night, derailed the so-called main event forever, and he *still* lost Aolani or Polunu to the other side, the victory would be a hollow one. Bolan played all-or-nothing stakes, regardless of the game.

He swept the field for targets, found one edging out from cover by the second car, to reach the first, and waited for the man to make his move. A glimpse of face told him that it was not Nahoa.

Never mind.

The Executioner would take what he could get.

The shooter made his move, and Bolan led him just a little, stroked his rifle's trigger once and sent a shot downrange.

The runner squawked, sounding exactly like a startled parrot, as he spun and hit the pavement on his backside, facing back the way he'd come. Another second, and he toppled over on his left side, shivered briefly and lay still.

Waiting in darkness, Bolan whispered, "Come on out. Let's get this done."

BOLAN SAW AOLANI huddled beside the first car that had entered the parking lot. She was trying her best to stay out of harm's way, but it was a crapshoot with so much high-velocity death in the air.

The quickest way to help her, Bolan reasoned, was to take out the rest of Nahoa's men and finish the fight. He was about to scan for targets, when a hand reached out toward Aolani from behind the car, groping to reach her.

Bolan fired a warning shot, gouging asphalt near Aolani's face and making her flinch. The questing hand withdrew, but almost instantly came back again. This time, the fingers snagged their target and began to drag the kicking, struggling woman out of sight.

The angle now precluded Bolan firing at the hand or arm behind it. Any shot he tried would rip through Aolani's skull before it found its mark. Instead, Bolan applied some physics and his knowledge of modern auto design, raising his sights to fix upon the gang car's left-rear fender.

Just about where he supposed the face of Aolani's captor ought to be.

Bolan fired three quick shots, shifting an inch or so each

time, to give his rounds a spread. The bullets cut long teardrop gouges in the fender, then punched through empty air to exit near the left taillight. He had no other target visible, but—

Aolani squealed and vaulted to her feet, released from the grip on her hair, bolting off into darkness. Bolan covered her, saw one of Nahoa's shooters rising from a crouch to cut her down and took the guy's head off around eye-level. By the time his body dropped, Aolani was out of sight and relatively safe.

Now it was time for mopping up.

With fourteen rounds remaining in his sniper rifle's magazine, Bolan saw no need for a headlong charge into the killing ground below. Conversely, every second wasted raised the likelihood that a police car might turn up, either routinely driving by, or summoned by some motorist who saw the firefight going on.

What Bolan couldn't do was try to detonate the fuel on either of the cars downrange. Polunu, presumably, was still inside one auto's trunk, and torching off the other ran a risk of setting its companion vehicle on fire.

He could encourage those who hid behind the cars to move, however, without sparking an inferno. All it should take was the high-powered gun in his hands and a working knowledge of physics.

Methodically, Bolan spent the last fourteen rounds in his clip punching holes through the cars, in one side and out the other. Detroit rolling stock grew more flimsy each year, despite safety improvements that consisted primarily of plastic, air in bags and microchip electronics. None of those could compare to a prototype Model T Ford, where stopping bullets was concerned. There was a reason why so many 1930s bandits drove away from shootouts with police and FBI agents, while modern vehicles were totaled by a low-speed fender-bender.

By his seventh shot, augmented from below by rhythmic bursts from Johnson's autocarbine, Bolan's hidden targets had begun to stir uneasily, feeling the reaper's red-hot breath upon their napes.

The first guy broke from cover in a crouching duck-walk, spraying SMG fire toward the slope that hid his tormentor. Bolan was pivoting to drop him, when Johnson stitched the shooter with a burst of 5.56 mm manglers that reduced him to a crumpled heap of flesh and tattered clothing.

That left four or five still fit to fight, by Bolan's count, and two of them emerged a heartbeat later, tearing off in opposite directions to confuse their unseen enemies. Bolan let Johnson have the runner nearest him, swinging his weapon to the right to track the other with his telescopic sight.

A stride or two before he would've reached concealing shadows, Bolan fired. His bullet closed the fifty-yard gap between sniper and target in one-twentieth of a second, ripped through fabric, flesh and bone without any appreciable loss of velocity and flattened the runner as if he'd been struck by Thor's hammer.

Three or four armed hostiles remained, with four rounds in the sniper rifle's magazine and Bolan's AK-47 waiting on the ground beside him.

It was plenty.

Johnson dropped another of the hostiles in his tracks, as Bolan swung back to the locus of the action. Even as that dying shooter fell, another came out firing from behind the first car, bellowing his futile rage and knowing that no quarter would be asked or granted.

Bolan and Johnson fired as one, the single round from Bolan's rifle shearing off the target's scalp, while Johnson's carbine punched four or five holes in his chest. Eerie silence fell over the scene, as the echoes of gunfire receded.

It was time to walk among the dead and make sure no survivors remained.

BOLAN SLUNG the PSG, picked up the Kalashnikov and descended the slope without taking his eyes off the parking lot's tableau of death. He circled to the right, Johnson cutting to the left as he replaced the spent clip in his Colt M-4 Commando.

Any member of the hit team still alive would have to show himself—and face their withering cross fire—within the next few seconds.

He heard Aolani calling to him from the outer darkness, moving closer, but he focused on the bullet-punctured vehicles. Distraction at this stage could be a fatal error, as experience had taught the Executioner on other battlefields.

Behind the first car, Bolan found Nahoa lying supine, one eye staring at the night sky overhead. The other eye was gone, together with a portion of his forehead and the brain his skull had once contained, all blasted into crimson mist by one of Bolan's probing shots into the left-rear fender.

After checking underneath the nearest car, and seeing Johnson sweep below the other, Bolan called out to the night, "Okay, Leia. We're finished here."

She ran to join him, then rushed past him to the second car and stood before its trunk. "Polunu's in here," she said, pointing. "We need to get him out."

Johnson looked for keys in the ignition, couldn't find them, but he *did* locate a switch beside the driver's seat, marked with the tiny picture of an open trunk. A moment later, Aolani was extracting Polunu from his claustrophobic prison, giving him the once-over like an ER nurse checking for visible trauma.

Bolan had already noted that the trunk lid and fenders were unscarred by bullets. Stepping aside from the happy reunion, he glanced toward the trunk's gaping maw and stopped short.

Where Polunu had reclined in darkness moments earlier, what looked like a crumpled Navy uniform now lay exposed, beside the second car's spare tire and folded jack. Bolan retrieved the shirt and turned it over in his hands, examining the various insignia.

The one that mattered was a shoulder patch, embroidered in light blue for contrast on a darker background. The patch depicted two stylized dolphins on the ocean's surface, facing inward toward the prow of an advancing submarine.

A worm of worry started gnawing at the back of Bolan's mind.

Six sailors missing from Pearl Harbor.

What was their assignment?

Circling past Aolani and Polunu to the second car's passenger side, Bolan opened the front door, then the glove compartment. Half a dozen maps were jammed together there. He drew them out, examined each in turn.

A road map for Oahu, and a Honolulu Street map.

Ditto Waikiki.

A more specific North Shore map.

And two on shiny paper, tourist maps.

One showed the layout of Pearl Harbor, while the other charted a hotel-resort called Turtle Bay.

Bolan could almost hear the click of pieces falling into place.

He only hoped that it was not too late.

10

Pearl Harbor, Oahu

The six men who approached Pearl Harbor Naval Base that
morning had the proper uniforms, bearing and attitude. They
also had the proper ID cards, created for one thousand dollars
each by Honolulu's most respected forger. Best of all, the
names printed on the ID cards actually belonged to Navy personnel stationed at Pearl.

As for the faces, with extreme buzz cuts and certain small,
cosmetic touch-ups, they were close enough to pass.

Or, so the six men hoped.

All six got through without a hitch, thanks to a hacker who
had fudged the records of their real-life counterparts to show
them out on two-day liberties, returning at the time and place
where Lanakila's men stood ready to present themselves. Once
past the gate, their first hurdle, the six shared a sensation of relief
but gave no sign that any other outcome had been contemplated.

This was not a time for weakness. None of Lanakila's
soldiers had the luxury of yielding to their nerves. So far, they
were on track for a successful mission.

But the toughest part, most potentially disastrous part of all,
was yet to come.

Turtle Bay Resort

SENTRIES WERE NOT a problem on arrival at the lavish Turtle Bay
Resort. Entry was unobstructed from Kamehameha Highway,

but the guests' parking lot was monitored by a resort employee in an open booth, stationed halfway between the highway and the heart of the resort. Before reaching the booth, Bolan had his choice of public parking lots on either side, maintained in strict accordance with Hawaiian law that opened every foot of beachfront to the public, night or day.

He parked the rented car, got out and locked it once his three companions had emerged into the brilliant sunlight, offset by a cooling breeze that wafted inland from the sea. They couldn't see the water yet but could hear surf splashing every now and then, the wind carrying the soft sound to their ears.

Bolan had done his homework, going in. He knew that Turtle Bay occupied Oahu's northernmost point, surrounding the world-famous Sunset Beach. It was accessible from east or west along Kamehameha Highway—and, at least in theory, from the sea. Its hotel towers contained 375 luxury guest rooms and twenty-six suites, while forty-two beach cottages and ocean villas placed lucky guests within spitting distance of the surf.

The resort also featured five miles of beachfront, two eighteen-hole championship golf courses, ten tennis courts, six restaurants, a spa, riding stables, a helipad for sightseeing tours of Oahu, plus mountain-bike and hiking trails that covered most of the resort's 880 acres. With thousands of guests in residence at any given time, Turtle Bay might be a tempting target for terrorists under normal conditions.

But this week wasn't normal.

Instead of celebrity golfers and camp followers, Turtle Bay was hosting top-ranked politicians, journalists, and others who had flocked to Oahu for the upcoming Pearl Harbor memorial ceremonies, scheduled to begin in one day's time. The synchronicity of that had Bolan on mental alert, but he still wasn't sure how the ceremonies might dovetail with Lanakila's planned main event.

An assault on Pearl Harbor itself, whether by land, sea, or air, was hardly feasible. The naval base was well defended and highly security conscious, its stationary defenses augmented by those aboard various warships in port and nearby. Would-be attackers faced a lethal list of hazards ranging from sentries with small arms to helicopter gunships, Navy fighter planes, cruise missiles, and the twenty-inch guns of U.S. battleships.

Superman might break through those defenses, but no one from Pele's Fire would survive the attempt.

An attack on Turtle Bay, with various statesmen and high-profile news folk in residence, would be simpler to accomplish—but even there, the chances of success were slim to none. With mainland dignitaries occupying the resort, police and federal agents would also be found on the grounds, escorting their charges under guard on the average forty-five-minute drive to and from Pearl Harbor. Employees would be double-checked, as they arrived and left, while the civilians granted access to the beachfronts would be under constant scrutiny.

None of those precautions could guarantee safety against a determined suicide attack, but Bolan still rated the chances of a hit team reaching any noteworthy targets as close to zero.

And still, something nagged him.

Surf's up. Fire from the sea.

Six U.S. Navy submariners kidnapped and presumably murdered.

For their uniforms, maybe?

It seemed preposterous, of course. But what else could it mean?

As Bolan and his three companions drifted farther into Turtle Bay Resort, he examined his knowledge of submarines. Each modern U-boat carried a crew of one hundred or so, but how many were actively working at any given time? What was the minimum number required to operate a submarine? To navigate? To make its weapons operational?

Bolan had no clear-cut idea.

This much, he knew: Pele's Fire had no submarine fleet, and even if it did, the boat could not slip past security at Pearl Harbor.

And Turtle Bay? How would a submarine offshore menace the huge resort, its personnel or guests, in concrete terms?

Short of a missile launching, could it pose a danger to the hotel towers or beach cottages?

Questions, to which the Executioner had no hard answers. Brognola would need to speak with someone in authority, someone who had the necessary information at his fingertips, to find out if the threat was even feasible.

If not, where did that leave Bolan and his three allies?

Checking out the grounds at Turtle Bay.

"Watch out for any weak points you can spot," he told them, going in. "We're handicapped, not knowing what to look for in advance. Polunu, if you see anyone who looks familiar from your old crew, sing out loud and clear."

"Don't worry," Polunu said. "If they see me, and they know me, you won't have to ask."

I hope not, Bolan thought, as he approached the epicenter of the posh resort.

North Shore, Oahu

WAITING, IN LANAKILA'S opinion, was the hardest part of any job.

His problem was that he'd run out of time, just when his world seemed to be on the brink of falling apart. The deal with Polunu and his lady friend, which was supposed to cure most of Lanakila's problems and reveal his enemies, had blown up in his face big-time. He'd lost Eddie Nahoa and nine other men whom he couldn't spare, while Polunu and Aolani had escaped. None of his enemies were even grazed by bullets, that he knew of, and to top it off, the pigs were turning up the heat on anyone who'd ever said a kind word about Pele's Fire.

Tough shit for them.

His hard-core members had gone underground when Lanakila had. A hundred men, in round numbers, and he'd lost nearly one-fifth of those in the past twenty-four hours. Much more of that attrition, and there'd be no army left for Lanakila to command.

So what?

The main event was coming, and it would make all the difference in the world.

He had been forced to move ahead on schedule, despite the massacre at Sacred Falls State Park. His team was trained and ready. They would never be so primed to strike again, and there might never be another equal target offered if he lived to be as old as Adam in the *haole* Bible.

It was now or never. This one day was all the opportunity he'd ever have to hit the blue-eyed bastards where they lived and leave a lasting mark on history.

The main event.

His unknown enemies had darkened Lanakila's outlook on the future, granted, but it was always touch and go, in his mind, what would happen after his strike team delivered their grand sucker punch. The optimistic part of Lanakila's mind had always imagined him sitting on a beach somewhere, attended by two or three adoring and grateful *wahines* who saw to his every need.

But maybe it wouldn't be like that, after all.

Maybe he'd be caught up in the frenzied manhunt that was bound to follow execution of his plan. If he was run down by the pigs, smart money said they'd kill him on the spot, for pure revenge, but if they hauled him in and held him in a cage for trial, then Lanakila's second-finest moment might occur in court.

Defendants were allowed to speak up for themselves under the *haole* law. If he was placed on trial, Lanakila could always represent himself. He didn't care about the old saying that a lawyer who defended himself had a fool for a client. Lanakila's murder trial—make that mass-murder trial—would be his final chance to shine, to get his message out there in the world before the *haoles* executed him or locked him up and threw away the key.

The thought of legal execution didn't trouble him. Hawaii had no death penalty statute, but since his crime was federal, involving military property and personnel, he would likely get the needle.

Death had always been part of the picture for Lanakila. Win or lose with Pele's Fire, he wasn't going to live forever. The important part of life was fighting for a cause. If there was time before the end, he would spread his message far and wide. Infect another native generation with the spirit of rebellion against *haole* rule over the sacred islands of Hawaii.

It wasn't immortality, exactly, but it was the best Lanakila could expect from life. He'd done his part, now all he had to do was wait and hope that his men, his sailors, would not let him down.

And waiting was the hardest part, damn it.

Always the hardest part.

Turtle Bay Resort

AFTER TWO HOURS on the ground, Bolan believed that he and his three companions had seen everything they needed to at Turtle Bay.

Granted, they hadn't toured the hiking trails or golf links, hadn't gone upstairs in either of the hotel towers to survey guest rooms, and hadn't booked a chopper flight around the place to view its various approaches from the air. They also hadn't played a doubles tennis match, gone swimming in the pool, or stopped for a massage.

But they had done the place, in recon terms, and as they moved back toward their vehicle, Bolan knew Turtle Bay would make a tempting mark for Lanakila's troops.

How would they strike?

Surf's up! Fire from the sea!

A dying bit of misdirection from a dedicated terrorist? Or did Bobby Niele's last words hold the key to Lanakila's main event?

Bolan still didn't know, but he'd decided it was time to share the burden of his personal uncertainty. Maybe Brognola or the team at Stony Man could put flesh on the bones of Bolan's brooding dread. Decide if anything remotely similar was even possible.

They were still a hundred yards from the visitors' parking

lot when Bolan broke off from the others, palmed his sat phone and speed-dialed Brognola's office in Wonderland, on Pennsylvania Avenue.

Brognola couldn't see the White House from his office window, but he always felt it lurking down the street. Favors and congratulations were dispensed from there, when things went well. And when they didn't, a whisper or stroke of a pen could slam doors on bright futures, aborting careers.

Brognola was a longtime player in D.C. He knew the angles and the risks as well as anyone. He could digest Bolan's suspicions and decide to act on them or not, as he saw fit.

But on Oahu, at Ground Zero, it would still be Bolan's choice. And to complete that choice, he needed help, ASAP.

The distant telephone rang once before Brognola picked it up. Instead of waking him, this time Bolan had caught him in the nadir of his working day, another hour or two remaining on the nine-to-five clock.

"Speak to me," Brognola said.

"What can you tell me about submarines?" Bolan inquired without preamble.

"They go underwater," Brognola replied. "If everything works right, they come back up again."

"I'm hoping for a little more detail," Bolan said.

"Sorry. In that case, I'd have to ask someone or search the Web. What are you looking for, specifically?"

"Security procedures," Bolan said. "Whatever ship-to-shore controls are normally in place. The bare-bones minimum personnel required to make one operational."

"Can't say I like the sound of this," Brognola said.

"I don't like thinking it," Bolan replied.

"Without specifics at my fingertips, I'm thinking that security ashore would be as tight as any other military standard. Fighters, bombers, tanks, whatever. When they're not in use, they're guarded, right?"

"I hope so."

"On the other hand…"

Brognola let it trail away, but Bolan knew what he was thinking.

On the other hand, specific vehicles might not be guarded individually, on a large and busy military base. They didn't post a guard on every APC or tank, of course, but there were always personnel around in daylight. After dark, there were sentries, patrols. Surveillance cameras and other gear would be engaged around the clock.

But, still…

"You think it's possible?" Brognola asked at last.

"I'm asking you."

"And I have no idea. I'll have to ask someone. Six men, you think?"

"I found one uniform they won't be using," Bolan answered. "I couldn't tell you whether it was one of the original six, or more likely something they picked up earlier, or a look-alike from a costume shop."

"No name tag, I suppose," Brognola said.

"Just the insignia for submarines."

"Okay, I'll check it out, but I can't promise when I'll have an answer for you. If nobody can help me at the Farm, I'll have to try the Pentagon."

"Good luck with that," Bolan commiserated.

"Hey, you're telling me." Brognola switched gears, saying, "Sounds like you've been keeping busy, since we talked last."

"I've been whittling," Bolan granted, "but I haven't found the CEO or pinned down any details on his final plans. Just supposition, so far, but it looks like Turtle Bay Resort."

"I've heard of that place," Brognola said. "Couldn't swing the loot to take the wife there, when we made it to the Islands, but it sounded nice. Isn't that where the VIPs are staying for tomorrow's bash?"

"Affirmative."

"Well, shit. I'd better get those questions asked and answered, then, before we have one messed-up luau on our hands."

"I'm standing by, whenever you get something," Bolan said.

"Okay," Brognola answered, and it was his turn to cut the link without goodbyes.

Bolan caught up with his companions, moving toward their car. He had to think of something that would rock Lanakila and his dwindling army to its core, delay their plans as long as possible, while Brognola worked out the probability of Bolan's gut hunch coming true.

He would be standing by for word from Washington.

But he would not be standing still.

THEY SAT IN THE CAR, windows down and a cool breeze blowing from the not-so-distant ocean, devising a strategy. Bolan was open to suggestions, and he said so.

"Well, we can't do anything at Pearl," Johnson said, stating the obvious. "If they've got something cooking at the base, I'm guessing the Navy can handle it."

Maybe, Bolan thought, but he said, "Agreed. I need to keep the pressure on Lanakila and his soldiers, then. The less time they have to think or move forward with plans, the better."

"Get out there and rattle some cages," Johnson said.

"I'd say so."

"Works for me," the surfer replied, "as long as we know who and where the targets are."

All eyes turned toward Polunu on that one. "Hey, wait, now," he said. "I don't know anything."

"You were inside for, what?" Aolani asked him. "Three years? Pretty much from the start, wasn't it?"

"But I wasn't a leader," Polunu said. "Their shit was all need-to-know, get it? I didn't get everything."

"Nobody asked you for everything," Bolan replied. "Give us something."

"Well, they have safehouses. Had them, anyway. I can't

say they're still using them, with what's been going on. You
want me to, I'll show you where they are, or were, but we
could drive all up and down Oahu, kicking doors and not find
anything."

"Can you make a list?" Bolan asked.

Polunu shrugged. "Don't see why not. I know half a dozen.
Where they used to be, at least. How do you want it?"

"Any around this area?" Bolan asked.

"One," Polunu replied.

"Then start off with the farthest place from Turtle Bay and
bring us back in this direction."

Bolan knew there were risks inherent in his latest strategy.
Polunu could be right about the safehouses, for one thing.
Lanakila might have closed them as a security precaution after
Polunu bailed from Pele's Fire, or he could've emptied them
when Bolan's blitz began.

If they got lucky, and the safehouses were occupied, Bolan
still ran the risks inherent during any combat operation. He
might lose his comrades, or he might be hurt or killed himself
before Brognola could respond to his inquiry on the submarine
issue. In that case, what would stand between Lanakila's private
army and the main event?

Nothing.

But Bolan felt an overwhelming need to do something, and
all that he could think of at the moment was to rattle Lanakila's
world with everything he had, keep Pele's Fire off balance if
he could, and thereby—maybe—toss a monkey wrench into the
inner workings of their master plan.

And failing that, if Lanakila made his score on schedule,
Bolan would hopefully be there to mop up the stragglers. He
couldn't guarantee that none of them would get away from him,
but he would do his best to see that didn't happen.

And his best, if Bolan did admit it to himself, was pretty
damned good.

"All done," Polunu said, handing back the pad and pen to Aolani.

She tore off the two sheets he had filled with addresses and handed them to Bolan.

"Like I said, these may all be dry holes," Polunu added.

"We'll soon find out," Bolan said as he read the list. Pointing, he turned and asked Polunu, "These are in order, starting with the farthest from our present point, backtracking so we wind up here again?"

"That's right."

"Okay. So, we'll be starting down the coast, at Barbers Point. What kind of place is that?"

"A normal house," Polunu replied. "One-story, with a basement and a little bit of yard in back. Carport instead of a garage. The neighborhood's not great, so anybody fits right in."

We'll see about that, Bolan thought, as he started the car, reversed out of the parking space and started back along the hundred-yard driveway to reach Kamehameha Highway heading south.

I guess we'll see.

11

Barbers Point, Oahu

Barbers Point, on the leeward shore of Oahu, was named for Henry Barber, the captain of a ship that wrecked along the coast in 1796. Construction of a lighthouse followed Barber's tragic accident, and land investors were not far behind. In the 1930s, the U.S. Navy leased part of Barbers Point from a private estate and later constructed a Marine Corps Air Station, ceded to the Navy proper during World War II.

When the Navy pulled up stakes it left behind a small Coast Guard facility, along with four golf courses, Kapolei Regional Park and a substantial block of private housing.

Bolan's target lay within the latter zone, as he approached on Farrington Highway, then turned off on H-95. Johnson rode the shotgun seat in the rented car, while Aolani and Polunu sat in the rear. Bolan would have preferred to drop their backseat passengers somewhere removed from the impending action, but Polunu was their navigator and Aolani balked at being left alone so soon after her kidnapping.

"A daylight raid," Johnson said. "We'll have to take precautions, like at Happy's place."

"I'm tryin' to tell you guys," Polunu said from the backseat, "there's most likely no one home. If it was me, I would've changed the safehouses around when someone bailed. I mean, like *I* did."

"Changing houses may not be that easy," Bolan told him. "Moving out's one thing, but where do you go next? When you need shelter, someplace for concealment, living on the street is not an option."

"You're the boss, man," Polunu answered. "I'm just saying."

"If you're right," Johnson said, "we should know it pretty soon."

H-95 turned into Malakole Street, and Bolan turned south onto Haunua, as Polunu had directed him. Two blocks, and then a left turn onto Komohana, slowing to sweep the north side of the street and find the fourth house on his left.

It was a single-story dwelling with a carport, just as Polunu had described. He had the color right, as well, a one-time pastel yellow that the tropic sun had faded to a sad off-white. There was an old Ford in the carport, but a drive-by couldn't tell them how long it had been sitting there.

"Would they run off and leave a car?" Johnson asked.

"Maybe," Polunu said. "They steal most of their rides, know what I'm saying? Maybe it's not running. Maybe they pulled out and squatters grabbed the place. There's no way I can tell you from out here."

"Once more around the block," Bolan said, "then we make a house call. Leia, you'll be at the wheel, waiting."

"I lost my gun," she said, sounding embarrassed. "I mean, when they—"

"You won't need one," Bolan interrupted. "Give us ten minutes, then drive around the block. If we're not out here by the second pass, clear out."

"But what if they—"

"If someone shows up while we're checking out the place, take off. We'll handle it and get in touch as soon as possible. Still have your cell phone?"

"No. They took it with the pistol, when I, um, when they—"

Bolan unclipped a cell phone from his belt and passed it to Aolani. "This is mine," he said. "Don't lose it. Don't make any calls for any reason. Clear?"

"I hear you."

On the second time around, he found a place to park at curbside, two doors from the target house. Bolan and Johnson had their missionary jackets on again, hiding a multitude of sins. As Aolani slid into the driver's seat of Bolan's rented car, leaving Polunu in the backseat, they walked up to the safehouse, stood to each side of the door, and Bolan rang the bell.

Nothing.

He heard it chime inside, a tinny sound, but no one answered on the second, third, or fourth ring. They could hear no sounds of movement from within, suggesting that a lurker was prepared to wait them out.

"Around back?" Johnson asked him.

"Might as well."

The small yard Polunu had described was fenced in chain link, shoulder high, with shrubs planted around the perimeter. No one had watered them for days, maybe even a week or more, and they were slowly dying under the Hawaiian sun.

The back door opened onto a kitchen—literally, since it was unlocked. Cautiously, Bolan and Johnson made their way inside, weapons revealed and ready to retaliate if they were ambushed. However, no gunfire erupted from the kitchen or adjacent rooms. Musty air told them the doors and windows had been closed tight for some time, with no air-conditioning to clear the smell.

"Long gone," Johnson said.

"We should check it, anyway."

Five minutes later, they were back together in the kitchen. Bolan didn't let his disappointment rattle him. He'd missed his quarry, but the next time could be different.

Back on the street, they moved in tandem to the rented car, Aolani retreating to the backseat, clearing Bolan's place behind the wheel.

"Nothing, I guess," Polunu said.

"Not this time," Bolan replied. "We'll check the other places, anyway."

"Likely a waste of time," said the defector.

"Maybe. But it's all we have right now,"

At least, until he heard from Brognola again.

Pearl Harbor

THE SIX INTRUDERS, bound by no legitimate assignments and expected nowhere, made their way directly to Pearl's firing range. There, each man signed out a sleek Beretta M-9 auto-loading pistol and a box of ammunition. The guns were loaded, and each man carried thirty-four spare cartridges.

By regulations, the pistols could not leave the firing range. David Likikia took care of that by going to ask the range master a question in his soundproof cubicle, shutting the door, then firing twice into his chest at point-blank range.

The corpse fit fairly well beneath the dead man's desk. With any luck, no one would notice it before they reached their final goal—and if somebody did, so what? A search by members of the Shore Police would center on the firing range and spread from there, taking two hours or more to reach the submarine pens.

It was more than enough time.

With pistols tucked into their waistbands, hidden by the loose tails of their camouflage-patterned BDU shirts, the invaders made their way from the firing range to the sub pens. They did not double-time or march in formation, did nothing at all to draw attention from the legitimate personnel whom they passed on their way. When meeting officers, they snapped off brisk salutes without a second's hesitation, and moved on.

Their target was the SSN *Newark,* a fast-attack submarine of the USS *Los Angeles* class. It measured 362 feet long from bow to stern, and thirty-three feet wide. It was built to pursue and destroy enemy ships or submarines, using torpedoes, but also carried a supply of cruise missiles with conventional high-explosive warheads for ship-to-shore combat.

It was perfect.

And, at the moment, it was unmanned.

A problem Lanakila's soldiers meant to rectify.

Their training for this mission, dubbed the main event, had been protracted and intense. Two members of the team, David Likikia and William Palokana, had been Navy submariners in another life, before they quit the service and discovered the gospel of revolution preached by Pele's Fire. With Navy manuals and training videos obtained from bootleg sources, they had schooled two dozen of their fellow militants in the techniques of handling and maintaining a *Los Angeles*–class submarine.

Of course, it would've been impossible to infiltrate Pearl Harbor with two dozen men. Six had been pushing it, but they were skilled enough to get the *Newark* out of port and out to sea. Once clear of Pearl, the sub would rendezvous with a selected surface vessel, and the other crew members would come aboard.

And, after that, the main event.

Likikia—now Seaman Owen Kila—half expected to be stopped before he reached the submarine. They had a story all prepared, about last-minute maintenance before the *Newark* sailed the next day, for the celebration of Pearl Harbor's hundred-something years of service as a U.S. naval base.

Before that party started, though, the *haoles* would be in for a surprise. The last, in fact, that some of them would ever have.

They reached the *Newark,* went aboard and made their way belowdecks without being challenged. Once below, the men fanned out to their assigned positions in the engine room and ship's control center. With hatches battened down and radios switched off for the duration, there would be no further contact with the outside world unless they willed it. Or, unless the Navy chose to sink them as they powered out of port.

It was a gamble, granted, but Likikia believed that they had everything to win, and nothing much at all to lose.

Maili, Oahu

THEY APPROACHED Maili from the south, along Kamehameha Highway, working their way back toward the Turtle Bay

Resort. Bolan was conscious of the posted speed limit, but matched his own speed to the flow of traffic, watching for police cars as he drove.

They still weren't hunted to the best of Bolan's knowledge. Not officially, at least. They'd left no witnesses who could describe them, place them at the scene of any crime. There was no reason for an all-points bulletin to flag their vehicle or prompt a stop, unless Bolan called some undue attention to himself along the way.

Maili was a midsized coastal town, on par with Nanakuli to the south, or Waianae to the north. The house they wanted was on Saint Johns Road, maybe a half mile from the nearest beach. Its sun-bleached, generally rundown neighborhood was marked by poorly tended palm trees, bicycles and battered surfboards in the yards, old cars that had been hauling human cargo to the water since the Beach Boys had their first chart-topper more than forty years ago.

One house was different. Still tired and faded, it displayed no evidence that anyone within had ever tried a recreational activity. It sat with curtains drawn against the daylight, nothing in the yard but sad, neglected grass. A shiny BMW in the driveway didn't fit the neighborhood. It seemed almost embarrassed to be caught slumming.

"I'd say somebody's home," Johnson offered.

"Looks that way," Bolan said, as he drove two doors beyond the target house and parked the car. "You want the front or back?"

"I'll ring the bell," Johnson replied.

"Okay. Give me a minute."

Bolan left the car, still in his missionary clothes, the folding-stock Kalashnikov wedged tight into his armpit. Aolani shifted automatically to take the driver's seat that he had vacated, still not at ease with it.

He crossed the street and cut across the nearest lawn, stepping around a child's tricycle that had only two wheels left, abandoned on the grass like roadside wreckage from a freeway accident. He cut between two houses, lost to sight from the one that concerned him, and soon confirmed what a glimpse from the street had suggested: the aging houses shared another strip of grass behind, one long backyard that served them all.

So much for privacy.

He took advantage of the builder's lapse, jogging along behind one house, and then another, until he had reached the one he sought. The back door, Bolan guessed, would open on the kitchen, possibly a laundry room or pantry, but with every window covered he could not be sure.

He checked his watch and waited, picturing Johnson's walk from the rented car to the front door. Bolan imagined him climbing the concrete steps, ringing the doorbell, waiting for an answer from within that might include a burst of automatic gunfire through the door and walls.

Another ninety seconds passed, then Bolan thought he heard a distant, muffled chiming sound. Was that the doorbell, or some busy housewife's kitchen timer, telling her the roast was done? Still listening for gunfire, knowing that he wouldn't have to strain his ears to catch it, Bolan slipped a hand inside his blazer, ready with the AK-47 if he needed it.

And suddenly, he did.

A clomping sound of heavy footsteps from within the target house had Bolan braced before the back door opened, flying wide to strike the wall behind it and rebound. A shirtless, sawed-off bodybuilder type stood on the threshold, brandishing a pistol in each hand. His body brought to mind a prison gym, beloved of cons who had nothing to do all day but bulk up for their next crime spree.

Before the two-gun desperado took a step, Bolan already had him covered. Guessing that a shouted warning would be wasted, Bolan fired two rounds and cut the shooter's legs from under him, 7.62 mm military rounds shearing through flesh to shatter his femurs and drop him, stunned, in the doorway.

Bolan still kept the wounded man covered, watching for

more movement beyond the open doorway as he advanced. He didn't look around for nosy neighbors, simply took for granted that the first shots would send at least one or two stampeding for their telephones.

As Bolan reached the fallen weight lifter and kicked his pistols out of reach, an Uzi burst from the direction of the front door silenced any further opposition in the not-so-safehouse. Johnson joined him, just as Bolan dragged the wounded man into a smallish kitchen and went back to close the door behind him.

"Say four minutes, max," the surfer told him.

"Right."

He grabbed a handful of the moaning shooter's curly hair and cranked his head back at a painful angle. When the eyes swam into focus on his face, Bolan said, "You have one chance to live. Will it be yes or no?"

"Say what?"

He shook the head to clear its fog, saw something like lucidity behind the eyes narrowed by pain.

"Listen!" Bolan snapped. "I ask questions. If you want to live, you answer. Get it?"

"Okay, brah."

"Where's Lanakila?"

"Shit, man, he don't tell us nothin'. Who you think I am, Eddie Nahoa?"

"No," Bolan replied. "I killed Nahoa last night. You want to join him?"

"No way, brah. But I can't tell you somethin' I don't know. That Joey's underground, okay? Says everything is need to know, and we ain't needy."

Bolan thought it had the ring of truth. "All right," he said. "Tell me about the main event."

The pain-filled eyes went wide, then narrowed back to slits again. "Big mojo, brah. He say you *haoles* gonna get a big fuckin' surprise."

"And what would that be?" Bolan pressed him.

"Need to know, man. Need to fuckin' know."

Bolan could see the shooter fading. Every heartbeat sent blood slithering across the floor from torn femoral arteries. The guy was busy dying now, and Bolan left him to it.

"Want to toss the place?" Johnson asked.

"No point," Bolan replied. "If Lanakila wouldn't tell them where he is, they couldn't draw a map."

"In that case," the surfer said, "I suggest we split."

They did, out through the back, letting the long dry yard clean the blood off the soles of their shoes. They had stopped leaving crimson footprints by the time they reached the sidewalk, but it made no difference.

Wherever Bolan went, throughout Oahu, he was leaving bloody tracks.

Department of Justice, Washington, D.C.

BROGNOLA WASN'T PSYCHIC, but sometimes he *felt* bad news before he answered ringing telephones. Maybe it was the fatalism ingrained by his decades as an FBI agent and counterterrorist. Maybe he'd simply grown up expecting the worst and seeing it delivered by a Universe that didn't seem to care.

The good guys won sometimes, of course, but always at a price. And nothing they achieved was ever carved in stone, except on funeral monuments.

No victory was ever absolute.

The bad guys never learned.

Brognola grabbed the telephone receiver midway through its second ring. It was his private line, which supported his premonition of bad news. The White House had his number, as did those in charge of Stony Man Farm and a handful of warriors at large in the world. No one who knew the number ever called to socialize, inquire about Brognola's health, or ask him out to lunch.

When that phone rang, someone was either dead, or else in urgent need of killing.

"Go," he said.

The voice of Barbara Price came back at him from Stony Man. "We have that info you requested on the submarines," she said.

"I'm listening."

"Okay. The standard crew consists of 133 officers and enlisted men. No women are currently assigned to submarine duty, based on privacy issues. They won't normally put out to sea with fewer than 127 men, but that covers three six-hour duty shifts. For some reason, in subs they claim a day is only eighteen hours long. Don't ask me why."

"Go on."

"At any given time, in other words, the boat—not ship—is being run by forty-four men. Some of those are cooks, medics, whatever. Cut them out of the equation, and from what I understand, a short-term skeleton crew could operate one of the *Los Angeles*–class fast-attack subs as long as they cover the critical stations."

"Which are?" Brognola prodded.

"Well, the ship control center needs two men handling the controls. And I mean literally handling the controls. Two guys sit there, turn wheels, flip switches, push some buttons, and the boat dives, surfaces, speeds up, slows down, changes direction, anything the captain wants it to do."

"Two guys," Brognola echoed, feeling his stomach twist into a knot.

"Of course, they'd need somebody in the engine room, a navigator, someone in command. The guys I spoke to say a six- or eight-man crew could do it, for a few hours at least. If they were able to board reinforcements, once they'd grabbed the boat and had it out to sea, so much the better."

"Weapons?" Brognola demanded.

"On the fast-attack subs, they've got MK-48 torpedoes, used for sinking other ships at sea. Aim them toward shore, they might blow up a pier or something, maybe burrow in the beach sand, but they can't go airborne. That leaves the TLAMs—Tomahawk Land Attack Missiles. They're long-range subsonic cruise missiles. Warheads are normally conventional, but in a pinch they can go nuclear."

"How many Tomahawks per submarine?"

"Um, let's see. On the average, 124."

"And there's a larger class of subs?"

"*Ohio* class," Price said. "They're the ballistic missile submarines, packing the Trident IIs. You need the stats on those?"

"No," he said. "You've told me what I needed. Thanks."

"That's it?"

"For now. I'll be in touch if anything develops."

Severing the link, Brognola sat behind his desk and tried to visualize the chaos that would follow launches of 124 cruise missiles from the sea, heading toward Oahu. Each missile flew at 550 miles per hour, with a maximum range of 1,500 miles. Conventional warheads carried 1,000 pounds of high explosives, while the nukes packed a 200-kiloton punch.

Brognola had no reason to suppose that any of the fast-attack subs based at Pearl were armed with nuclear warheads. As for the Tridents, if a gang of terrorists seized one of *those* U-boats, the whole damned world could soon go up in flames.

Or mushroom clouds.

Bolan was waiting for his callback on Oahu, and Brognola didn't want to stretch it out unnecessarily. He wasn't sure, as yet, that Bolan had the real threat pegged for Pele's Fire. But if he did, the Navy would be squealing soon.

They couldn't lose a submarine, with all those Tomahawks, and fail to notice it.

Scowling, Brognola reached out once more for the telephone.

Makaha, Oahu

THE HOUSE ON NOHOLIO Road, within a stone's throw of the Sheraton Makaha Golf Club, wasn't upper-crust by any stretch of the imagination. It was one of those you might find advertised as a fixer-upper or a starter home, for tenants who were short on cash but well supplied with optimism.

Bolan had suspected it was vacant when he made his drive-by. There was no car in the driveway, no garage to hide one, and the last person to leave the place had not been interested enough to push the screen door shut, much less to draw the curtains.

Still, he checked it out, with Johnson backing him, and Aolani waiting in the rented car with Polunu and the extra guns. When no one answered the doorbell, they walked around to the back and broke in through the kitchen, fairly quietly. It took a minute, maybe less, to verify that there was no one home. A layer of dust suggested that the last tenants had left some time ago.

"One out of three," Johnson observed, as they evacuated through the back door, circling toward the street.

"And nothing much to show for that one," Bolan said.

The surfer shrugged. "Two guys who won't be celebrating Lanakila's main event, at least."

"We need more than a body count," Bolan replied. "If I can't find out what he has in mind and put a stop to it, the rest has all been wasted."

"At least the other side will know that they were in a fight," Johnson said.

"That's no consolation if they win it."

"I see your point."

They cleared the backyard and were halfway to the car when Bolan's sat phone buzzed against his hip.

It had to be Brognola. Knowing that, he palmed the phone and asked, "What have you got?"

"Bad news and worse news," the man from Washington said.

Bolan kept moving toward the car but slowed his pace.

"I'm listening," he said.

"The bad news," Brognola continued, "is that half a dozen well-trained men *can* run a submarine short-term. It sounds like they could mobilize the weapons, too. Most of it's automated nowadays. Somebody says 'Fire Tomahawks.' Somebody else flips switches, pushes buttons, and they're gone. Long-term, it wouldn't work. There's too much maintenance, they couldn't handle the repairs and life support, whatever. But for several hours, if they don't screw up at the controls, its feasible."

"Okay." A lead weight settled in the pit of Bolan's stomach.

"Also, there's a possibility that they might take on reinforcements somewhere, once they had the boat in hand. Most likely ship-to-ship at sea, from what I understand."

Another problem. Bolan hadn't thought about a rendezvous at sea.

"So, what's the worse news?" he asked, dreading Brognola's response.

"Well, now, it seems the problem is no longer theoretical. I was about to call you when I heard this through the grapevine, then I had to call around and pull some heavy-duty strings to get the confirmation. Right now, it's as hush-hush as holy hell, and Washington is hoping that it stays that way."

"Tell me."

"They've got a fast-attack sub missing, out of Pearl. The Pentagon's still playing catch-up, but it looks like someone walked on-base with fake IDs, picked up some small arms from the firing range, took out the range instructor so he couldn't interfere, then made off with SSN *Newark*. Can you freaking believe it?"

"If it happened," Bolan said, "then I believe it."

"Right. So, anyway, it's out there, headed God knows where. The Navy's scrambling, using every trick they have to track it down. Matter of time, they tell me, but meanwhile, the *Newark* has more than a hundred Tomahawks on board. The hijackers could fire them all before somebody zeroes in and drops a depth charge on their ass."

"They won't just fire at random," Bolan said.

"You think not?"

"I'll bet money on it," Bolan answered. "Any odds you want."

"Okay, why won't they just start firing missiles if they're cornered?"

"Because," Bolan said, "they've got a nice fat target waiting for them, and they don't have far to go."

"You know something I don't?" Brognola asked.

"So far, it's guesswork," Bolan told him. "Let me check it out, first. If I'm right, you'll be the second one to know."

"Second? Who's first?"

"The hijackers," Bolan said, then he broke the link.

"What's up?" Johnson asked. "Are we going somewhere else?"

"Your place," Bolan said. "Then, we need a good, fast boat."

Waialua Bay, Oahu

"I KNOW A GUY," Johnson said. "I'm telling you he won't mind if we take his boat out for a little spin."

"And what if we don't bring it back?" Bolan asked.

"He'd be pissed," Johnson replied. "But will it matter?"

Bolan saw the surfer's point. If they were killed trying to stop a hijacked Navy submarine, it wouldn't matter to them in the least if Johnson's so-called friend was furious about his boat. If they survived, but lost the boat somehow, Bolan imagined Brognola's secret slush fund would make up the difference.

"Okay," he said. "So, where's the dock?"

They had come in on Farrington Highway, then followed Johnson's directions for a left turn onto Olohio Street, to pick up Crozier Drive along the coast. That quickly changed into Waialua Beach Road, led them into the town of Waialua, and around the large Puuiki Cemetery.

Everywhere they went, Bolan could see the ocean, but it was a boat he needed now, not open water without means to cross it.

"Coming up," Johnson assured him. "Take a left on Cane Haul Road, up here, and go across the bridge."

A moment later, they were passing over a finger of Waialua Bay, water below them, as well as on both sides. Aolani's reflection in the rearview mirror looked uneasy, whether with the bridge or their expanding mission, Bolan couldn't say.

"And up here, just ahead, you'll find a road down to the water," Johnson told him. "On your left."

Bolan saw it, braked and followed the narrow two-lane blacktop to a small, hidden marina. Johnson directed Bolan to an empty gravel parking lot with room for half a dozen cars, at most. Two piers extended from the shore into the bay, stout ropes securing two sleek cabin cruisers, one sailboat and one speedboat.

"That's ours," Johnson said, pointing toward the nearest cabin cruiser as they piled out of the car. "The *China Girl*."

"Your friend likes Asian women?" Aolani asked.

"I'm pretty sure he's gay," Johnson replied, and flashed a grin. "Sometimes a name is just a name."

"I ought to tell you, I get seasick," Polunu said to no one in particular.

Bolan was lifting two fat duffels out of the rental's trunk. During their stop at Johnson's place, they had bagged every weapon they could think of that might help them in a surface duel with a submarine.

"It doesn't matter," Bolan told Polunu. "You're not coming with us."

"Oh." From the expression on his face, Bolan couldn't decide if Polunu was relieved or disappointed. Finally, he bobbed his head and said, "Well, thanks. Sorry I couldn't help you more, and all."

"You did enough," Bolan replied. "The hard part, now, for you, is getting lost. No matter how it goes down on the water, there will still be guys from Pele's Fire hanging around. And you won't be their favorite character."

"No sweat," Polunu said. "I was thinking someplace in the desert might be good, where I can see them coming from a few miles off. Like in the movies, eh, brah?"

"Right. Good luck with that."

Aolani stepped close to Polunu and placed a comforting

hand on his shoulder. "You'll be okay," she told him. "If I don't see you again—"

"You'll see him," Bolan interrupted her. "You're staying back, too."

She spun to face him, anger flaring. "What?"

"You heard me. Johnson and I will handle this. On the water, when it hits the fan, you'd just be in the way."

"You mean, I went through all of this for nothing?"

"No," Bolan replied. "You went through it to help Polunu, then you helped me. You've done your job twice over. Cut yourself some slack. Be glad your part is done and you're alive."

She turned to Johnson, with a pleading look. "Ron, please! I need to see the end of this."

"This *is* the end, Sunshine," Johnson informed her. "All that's left is fishing, and they may not bite. We'll either find that sub and stop it, or we won't. Whichever way it plays, we don't need anybody else to go down with the ship."

They went aboard the *China Girl,* and Johnson made his way up to the flying bridge. A moment later, Bolan heard the boat's twin engines grumbling aft. Was Johnson's friend free with the cabin cruiser's keys? Was there a nameless friend, at all?

Bolan dismissed the questions from his mind and concentrated on the hunt that lay ahead of them.

Polunu helped cast off the bow and stern lines that secured the cabin cruiser to the pier, but Aolani hung back by the car, her arms crossed and shoulders hunched, as if to face a chilling breeze.

The afternoon was warm and bright as Johnson took them out to sea. It might be dark, or a new day, when they returned.

If they returned.

Bolan had never given much thought to a burial at sea, but he supposed that in the heat of action, it was all the same. Fight hard until the final bitter moment, go down swinging at the last.

And take as many of the bastards with you as you could.

12

Off Pupukea, North Shore, Oahu

Joey Lanakila's cabin cruiser, *Die Hard,* wasn't stolen. It was
twenty-eight years old, and he had purchased it with cash he
got from Happy Kiemela, thirteen months before. Since then,
the boat—named for his favorite film—had been repainted,
patched where it was leaking at the bow, and had its engines
overhauled to maximize its cruising speed.

Beyond that, it was pretty much as Lanakila had discovered
it, abandoned by its dead-beat owner at a Waikiki boatyard. It
had been more convenient for the lot's owner to sell it off than
break it up for salvage, so the deal was struck.

Now Lanakila was at sea with twenty handpicked soldiers who
had pledged their lives to Pele's Fire and victory. Nineteen of
those were trained to work aboard a submarine and would accompany him to his rendezvous with destiny. The twentieth would
take *Die Hard* back to her berth and wait for further orders.

Which, Lanakila realized, would likely never come.

He was a realist, no matter what his critics thought. Nothing
he did this day would spark a revolution among island natives
who were too fat and complacent to risk losing what they had
for something as ephemeral as pride. Lanakila did not expect
the masses to rise up and follow him.

It would've been impossible, in any case, since he expected
to be dead.

By now, he knew the U.S. Navy would be tracking its lost

submarine. He had enough time for the meet at sea, to board his crewmen and proceed to Turtle Bay, but there was no doubt in his mind that sub-chasers would overtake the *Newark*.

But they would not overtake it soon enough.

Before they found him, Lanakila told himself, the main event would be enshrined in history.

What happened after that was immaterial.

The sub-chasers might call for his surrender. If they did, he would refuse. If they did not, the end result would be the same. Depth charges. High explosives blasting shock waves through the sea until the *Newark*'s hull ruptured and all aboard it drowned.

Or, he could surface for a last-ditch fight. The *Newark* had torpedoes, and he didn't necessarily need all the Tomahawk cruise missiles for his ship-to-shore assault. Suppose he only fired off sixty, eighty, or a hundred of them, kept the rest for fighting ship to ship with those who hunted him?

It would be glorious.

But in the end, he knew there would be no escape. Not if he sank a dozen Navy ships, or two dozen. They would be after him with cruisers, battleships, dive-bombers—anything it took to punish Lanakila and his crew for their insult to *haole* dignity.

The men he'd chosen to accompany him on the *Newark* were prepared to die. They'd written wills, said their goodbyes to anyone who mattered in their lives without explaining what it meant, exactly. All of them were outcasts when he met them. Most had no real families and claimed no friends outside of Pele's Fire.

They would be martyrs for the cause.

If someone else should come along next month, next year, five years from now, and build a movement on the ashes Lanakila left behind, so much the better. If they didn't, he'd still have the satisfaction to die cursing *haoles* with his last breath, knowing that he'd hit them where it hurt the most.

Right in their egos.

Live on CNN.

He pictured fury in the Oval Office, curses barked at sniveling subordinates who stood with eyes downcast and took it all, praying to keep their jobs. Lanakila pored over imagined headlines, saw the talking heads on television grim faced in their shock at his accomplishment. He smelled their anguish, sweeter than the scent of hyacinth.

Imagine the disruption at the Pentagon, in the Department of the Navy! What about the descendants of the *haole* bastards who had first "discovered" the Hawaiian Islands, then invaded them with guns and missionaries?

Chickens coming home to roost, the saying was.

Off Waimea Bay, North Shore

"GOOD WAVES TODAY," Johnson said. "Wish I was out there riding them."

Bolan glanced toward the shore, a half-mile distant. He saw surfers—little more than dark specks on the water at that distance—lining up in ranks to catch the next wave rolling toward the beach.

"Want me to drop you off?" he asked.

"I didn't bring my board," Johnson replied, and shrugged. "Some other time."

Was that a hint of optimism in the aging surfer's voice, or simple fatalism?

Did it even matter?

Bolan turned back to his task, arranging weapons in the cockpit of the *China Girl*. He'd started with the heavy-hitter first, an FIM-92 Stinger RMP shoulder-launched surface-to-air missile. Designed for dropping aircraft from the skies, with 270 confirmed kills at last count, the Stinger boasted a range of 5,000 yards. Its missile used a two-stage solid rocket motor and carried a 6.6-pound high-explosive warhead. Bolan knew that while the Stinger was specifically designed for killing planes and helicopters, its RMP feature—short for reprogrammable microprocessor—allowed its use against earthbound or seagoing targets, as well.

Next up came three M-72 LAW disposable antitank weapons, each plastic expandable tube preloaded with a 66 mm HEAT warhead—short for High-Explosive Anti-Tank. The total package weighed eight pounds and had a maximum range of 1,000 yards, though its true effective range for a moving target was less than 200 yards.

The HEAT rounds contained explosive shaped charges, focused by a void within the charge itself to create a very high-velocity jet of molten metal that can punch through solid armor. Most manuals claimed penetration of armor 150 to 250 percent thicker than the diameter of the charge, but some made extravagant claims of 700-percent penetration. In Bolan's personal experience, the effectiveness of HEAT rounds depended on range, angle of impact and whether the projectile was spinning when it struck the target.

Aside from the three LAW rockets, Johnson's stash had also given up two Russian RPG-7s. The weapon's projectile was a bulky muzzle-loaded HEAT round weighing 4.5 pounds. Its effective range was listed as 300 yards, but battlefield tests showed few planned hits beyond one-third of that distance. With standard rounds, a decent hit could penetrate twelve inches of armor.

And, unlike the disposable LAWs, the RPG could be reloaded. Johnson's stash included twelve extra rockets for the two vintage launchers, giving them seventeen chances to breach the *Newark*'s hull.

Assuming that they ever found the sub, or got within range.

The rest of their weapons were small arms, ranging in size from a Stoner M63A1 light machine gun in 5.56 mm, down through assault rifles and sidearms, to thermite and fragmentation grenades. The latter would only be useful if they had to board the *Newark,* and if it came to that, Bolan supposed they were as good as dead.

The LAW rockets and RPGs would be their best bet, he

decided. While the U.S. Navy didn't advertise design details of its various ships, Bolan knew that nuclear subs could descend well below eight hundred feet. Their hulls were thick enough to withstand the crushing pressure at such depths, and he had no realistic hope of sinking the *Newark* with RPG rounds, but a Stinger might just do the trick if he played his cards right.

"What were you planning to do with a Stinger, Johnson?"

The surfer smiled. "You ask that now?"

"You're right. Forget it."

"Do you think we have enough, there?"

"For a submarine?" Bolan considered it, and shrugged. "Depends on how we find it, *if* we find it. Catch them on the surface, I believe we can do damage with the Stinger, maybe make it worse with LAWs and RPGs before they dive. The main thing is to stop them from launching any Tomahawks inland."

"It's a big ocean out here, friend," Johnson replied.

"We know their target," Bolan answered. Thinking to himself, I hope we do. "All we can do is get on station and patrol. Hope they come up for air."

"I don't suppose those Tomahawks can launch while they're submerged?"

"Most likely," Bolan answered. "But we've got a green crew on their maiden voyage, hyped up for a cause. I'm betting they'll want to see their target, maybe even show themselves to prove they pulled it off."

"Ego. It gets 'em every time."

"Let's hope so," Bolan said, and turned back to the preparation of their arsenal.

"YOU EVER THINK about retiring from the business?" Johnson asked, as they churned through the waves toward Turtle Bay.

"I never thought it *was* a business," Bolan said.

"Because you take no profit from it?" Johnson smiled and shook his head. "You know somebody does. All wars are economic and political. It's not just right or wrong."

"If you believe that," Bolan said, "what are you doing here, right now?"

"I spent the better part of thirty years running around the world and killing bad guys for my government," Johnson replied. "Or for the highest bidder, which was always *someone's* government. They always had a good reason why Mr. X and all his followers should die, you know? The marks were Communists or fascists, revolutionaries or reactionaries, enemies of this or that. I swallowed it because I liked the action. Needed it to feel like I was living. Then, one day, I staggered out of bed, picked up my gun and realized I didn't want to do it anymore."

"You didn't throw the guns away," Bolan observed.

"Hell, no. I woke up tired of fighting, bro, not tired of living."

"I'll repeat my question, then—what are you doing here, right now?"

"Retirement's not all it's cracked up to be," Johnson replied. "Don't get me wrong. I love the free time and the surfing. I made some investments in my old life that will keep me liquid for the rest of this one, with a chunk of change to spare. But sometimes, doing nothing much gets old. Know what I mean?"

"I've never tried it," Bolan said.

"It may not suit you. My advice to you, one war dog to another, make sure that you really want whatever you start wishing for. Because it might come true, and if your choice was just some half-assed whim, you're well and truly screwed."

"I'm doing this right now," Bolan replied, "because the opposition isn't civilized. That sounds like crap, I guess, with everything that civilized societies get up to every day, but I apply my own standards. The system only works if there are certain basic rules. The predators will never be extinct, but they can be controlled to some extent. I thin the pack, and maybe help a few of those who can't or won't fight for themselves."

"You're not a Darwinist," Johnson said.

"Not if that means standing by and watching psychopaths

run rampant when I have the means to stop them. Not if it means giving up on any trace of personal responsibility."

"We make an odd team," Johnson said. "You're bound by duty. I got bored."

"In this case," Bolan said, "I'm less concerned with motives than results."

"Can't promise anything," Johnson replied, "except a good fight if we find that submarine."

"The good fight," Bolan said, "is all that anyone can do."

Off Kawela Bay, North Shore

JOEY LANAKILA WAITED on the *Die Hard*'s flying bridge, scanning the sea through field glasses he'd purchased at an Army-surplus store. The glint of sunlight on the water's surface drove needles into his eyes, but Lanakila kept sweeping the horizon, waiting for his first glimpse of the hijacked submarine.

He offered up a prayer to Pele that it would arrive before the Navy came in search of it, with battleships, destroyers, and the rest. His little crew aboard the *Die Hard* wouldn't last five minutes against warships; even standard Coast Guard cutters would outgun them.

But, if they could all board the submarine…

His head began to throb, a pulsing pain behind his eyes at first, then spreading to his temples. Lanakila was prepared for the migraine. He took an inhaler from his pocket, thrust its spout into his left nostril and pressed the plunger with his thumb, inhaling deeply as the medication burst into his sinuses.

The palliative effect was not immediate, but he could feel it working within minutes, damping down the pain, even as sour dregs of medicine dripped into the back of his throat. He was restricted to one blast per day, on doctor's orders, but had two more of the small inhalers in his pockets, just in case.

Lanakila wouldn't let something as mundane as a headache spoil the main event.

Not even if it killed him.

"There it is!" one of his crewmen shouted, pointing off to starboard.

Lanakila cursed and turned in that direction with his field glasses. He should've been the first to spot the submarine. It was his right, as planner of the exercise and the commanding officer of Pele's Fire.

But never mind.

He saw it now, rising like some Leviathan of ancient times from the Pacific depths, and that was all that mattered. Water streamed off of the *Newark*'s conning tower, decks and swollen-looking flanks.

The ballast tanks, he told himself, trying to feel as if he was a true part of the crew, instead of an intruder.

When the sub had fully surfaced, Lanakila steered the *Die Hard* on an interception course. The transfer was inevitably awkward, but his crewmen did their best, securing lines, then leaping from the cabin cruiser to the sub's glistening deck. One nearly slipped and rolled into the sea, but others saved him, and the rest—including Lanakila—made it safely to the submarine.

Rick Konani stayed aboard the *Die Hard,* as agreed, manning the bridge as lines were cast off, waving almost sadly as his friends trooped down below decks on the sub. By the time the hijacked Navy boat submerged, the cruiser was already churning toward the coast, where Konani would return it to its dock before he vanished underground.

"Ready to try her out?" Lanakila asked his three companions in the sub's command center.

"Yes, sir!" they snapped as one.

"Bring her around," he said. "We'll see how the torpedoes work."

All this had been rehearsed, as much as possible, until it seemed that they knew everything they had to know. Technology would do the rest, or so he hoped.

Two of his men in the bow prepared the Mk-48 torpedo for

firing. The deadly fish weighed more than 3,400 pounds, but machines moved its bulk from cradle to firing tube, pausing while human hands armed the 650-pound high-explosive warhead. At Lanakila's order, the torpedo burst from its tube and sped in pursuit of the *Die Hard*.

Lanakila knew the military specs for the Mk-48. Officially, it had a five-mile range, skimmed through the water at 32 mph, and could be used at depths greater than 800 feet. Civilian sources gave the fish more credit, claiming speeds of 90 mph and ranges exceeding thirty miles.

It didn't matter, in this case.

The *Die Hard* was less than two miles distant when Lanakila sent the Mk-48 in its wake. He watched through the periscope, counting down the seconds in his head, until a waterspout erupted at the cabin cruiser's stern, followed immediately by a shattering explosion.

Lanakila didn't actually see the *Die Hard* sink. Instead, when the smoke cleared, the cabin cruiser simply wasn't there. An offshore breeze wafted the smoke in toward the beach, where he supposed some neighbor would've heard the blast and would soon telephone the Coast Guard or police.

So be it.

They were already too late, and simply didn't know it yet.

Off Turtle Bay, North Shore

"I HOPE YOU'RE RIGHT about this," Johnson said, as he surveyed the gently rolling sea a mile offshore from Turtle Bay Resort.

"They had the map," Bolan replied, but he'd already started second-guessing what the map of the resort might signify. "And if I'm wrong, it all comes down to guesswork. Pick a target somewhere on the coast and go for it."

"I hear you, bro. But I've been thinking."

"And?"

"What if the sub itself's the main event?" Johnson asked.

"Making off with it that way took nerve and lots of preparation. What if Lanakila wants to ransom it, or even sink it, as a 'Fuck you' to the *haole* government?"

Bobby Niele's dying words echoed in Bolan's head.

Surf's up. Fire from the sea.

"If that's their game, we'll get a call," Bolan replied. "I have a contact who'll be privy to demands if any are received. Meanwhile, if they wanted to destroy the sub, they could've put a bomb on board at Pearl. I'm thinking that they didn't steal a megaweapon just to sink it in the ocean."

"Yeah, I guess it doesn't make much sense. But if they turn up somewhere else..."

"I know," Bolan said. "But there's nothing we can do about it. They could surface anywhere around Oahu, or move on to one of the adjacent islands. We just have to play the hand we're dealt. Go with the evidence."

"I used to fudge a lot, when I was in the life," Johnson said. "Down toward the end, I couldn't swear I tagged the right guy half the time, you know? The sides got all confused. One day, we're trying to put druggies out of business. Two days later, we're protecting loads of shit because the smugglers are on *our* side. I got tired of it and started doing my own thing. Nobody seemed to mind much when I finally retired."

"And they just let you?"

"Well, there was some disagreement on the subject," Johnson granted, smiling. "One of my employers sent some guys to talk me out of it. They didn't fare well, and the next crew wasn't any better. Finally, we came to an agreement. They leave me in peace, and I forget about the shit we used to pull. Which, by the way, I've written down and stashed with lawyers in a half a dozen different time zones."

"Life insurance," Bolan said.

"It's worked, so far."

"And what if this goes south?"

That got a laugh from Johnson. "I was thinking about that," he said, "when we shipped out. How funny it would be if I got snuffed on this deal, and it put my old crew underneath the spotlight."

"So?"

"So, screw 'em," Johnson said. "I never really liked them anyway."

"Your turn," Bolan said, handing Johnson the binoculars. "I need to use the head."

"It's on your left, below, next to the galley."

Bolan was exiting the cabin cruiser's head and moving toward the companionway when Johnson called down from the flying bridge, "I think we've got something."

Rushing to join him, Bolan took the field glasses and aimed them aft, in the direction Johnson pointed. First, he seemed to see the ocean's surface swell, as if a giant bubble was about to burst, then came the *Newark*'s conning tower, rising from the deep.

"Ahoy, mate!" Johnson said, beside him. "Thar she blows!"

13

"We're there, sir," the *Newark*'s navigator said, turning to face Lanakila with a narrow smile.

The navigator wore blue coveralls, an outfit that the *haole* Navy called a *poopy suit*. Lanakila and the other crew members all wore the same outfits, for comfort and convenience—no snagging on equipment in close quarters.

"You're sure?" he asked the navigator, lowering his normal voice to give it more authority.

"Yes, sir!"

He raised the periscope, much larger than it seemed in any of the movies he had seen, and scanned the shoreline to the west. He saw surfers, swimmers, sunbathers, palm trees, nothing that identified the place as Turtle Bay Resort so far.

Another small rotation to his left, and Lanakila saw umbrellas, tables and recliners lined up on the deck beside a swimming pool. Behind the pool, rising in monolithic splendor toward the cloudless sky, was the main bloc of hotel rooms. A scan back in the opposite direction showed him cottages along the beach, some tennis courts and a parking lot.

"Okay," he told his men in the command center. "Prepare to surface."

Everything aboard the sub was a two-stage process. He couldn't simply dive or surface, for example, without giving orders to prepare: filling or emptying the *Newark*'s ballast tanks, securing any hatches that were opened on the surface, lowering the periscope, alerting men in various compartments on the sub, so that they weren't thrown to the deck or into bulkheads.

"Surface," Lanakila said a moment later, watching as his throttleman and planesman handled their controls. One gave the sub's speed a nudge; the other made adjustments to the forward planes, or fins, and made the sub rise toward the surface.

Lanakila felt it rising, had to brace himself with one hand on the chart table to keep from staggering across the cramped command center. He knew when they were riding on the surface, felt it in his legs and stomach as the *Newark* rolled and shifted with the action of the waves outside.

When they were steady, more or less, he piped an order to the weapons room. "Start arming Tomahawks," he commanded. "Have them ready to fly on my order."

A tinny voice came back, asking, "How many, sir?"

"How many have you got?" he countered.

"Well, um, plenty, sir. A lot."

"You'd best get busy, then. I want them all on standby."

"Yes, sir!"

Lanakila killed the link, lowered the periscope and climbed the conning tower's ladder to release the topmost hatch. His roost atop the tower corresponded to a surface vessel's flying bridge, allowing Lanakila to feel the brisk wind in his face and eyeball the sea for 360 degrees.

After a quick glance to the north and south, checking for Navy ships approaching, Lanakila concentrated on the lush skyline of Turtle Bay Resort. He pictured all the fat, rich *haoles* waddling around in there with trophy wives or girlfriends, some of them relaxing on vacation, many others getting ready for the ceremonies at Pearl Harbor. They had come to celebrate the *haole* conquest of Hawaii, and to mourn the wartime deaths of *haole* sailors who should never have been on Oahu in the first place.

What Lanakila did this day would not release the *haole* death grip on Hawaii. It might be too late for that, for all he

knew. But he was doing something, while most Polynesian nationalists sat in "study groups" and talked their lives away.

Belowdecks, Lanakila's men were priming Tomahawk
cruise missiles for flight. They would be using TERCOM—the
terrain contour matching navigation system—wherein each
missile's radar system "saw" terrain as it flew over and compared the landscape to a map stored in its memory. TERCOM
improved accuracy over the older inertial navigation system—
INS—and allowed Tomahawks to fly at lower altitudes, outwit-
ting defensive radar.

Not that it mattered, with this sitting duck of a target.

They hardly needed to aim for the high-rise hotel blocs, but
Lanakila meant to use every bit of the technology at his disposal.
He'd make the hit perfect, and massive, with no room for error.

There were bound to be survivors, of course, but Lanakila
didn't mind. Their halting, tearful stories on TV would go far
toward spreading fear among their *haole* countrymen. Unwit-
tingly, they would be serving Joey Lanakila's cause.

How could he ask for more?

"YOU'RE SURE it's the right U-boat?" Johnson asked. "I don't
see any name or numbers showing."

"No, there wouldn't be," Bolan replied.

"No chance the Navy sent another sub up here to look around?
Maybe they got your warning and decided it was worth a check?"

"We could sit back and wait until they fire the Tomahawks,"
Bolan said.

"Man, this bites."

"It does," Bolan confirmed. The Stinger lay beside him,
near his right foot, with the RPGs lined up to his left.

"I *really* hate to do this, when we can't be sure," Johnson said.

"Give it a minute," Bolan said.

"But they could fire the Tomahawks from underwater,
couldn't they? I read somewhere that they can do that."

"Probably." The warrior kept his eyes glued to the field

glasses, examining the submarine as water sluiced back from its decks and swollen ballast tanks.

"Well, that'd be the safe way, wouldn't it?" Johnson asked. "Why pop up and show yourself, when half the Navy must be looking for you?"

"Everywhere but here," Bolan replied.

"Jesus."

"Hang on," Bolan advised.

Johnson had glasses of his own, shifting from study of the submarine to long scans of the beach and swimming pool at Turtle Bay.

"I can't tell if they've even seen it yet," he said. "I mean, they're swimming, surfing, having lunch and drinks, like nothing's happening."

"Nothing *has* happened, yet," Bolan reminded him.

"Oh, yeah? I'll tell you something, if I was out riding waves some morning, and a goddamned submarine came out of nowhere, I believe I'd notice it and take a second look, at least."

"That's you," Bolan said. "Don't compare yourself with people on vacation who were never trained observers in the first place. They see nothing but their sandwich, or their cocktail, or the tight bikini walking by. If they look out to sea at all, they register the surfers close to shore for ten or fifteen seconds, then switch off."

"They wouldn't last five minutes in the field," Johnson replied.

"That's why they're never *in* the field. Most of them don't know that the field exists."

"Maybe they're better off, you know?"

Before he could respond, Bolan saw movement at the apex of the black sub's conning tower. Not the rising hatch, which was invisible from where he stood, but rather a man's head and upper torso, levitating into view as if by magic.

"Here's someone," he told Johnson.

The man had his back turned to Bolan. He wore a standard Navy poopy suit, like any other submariner, but his hair seemed longer than regulations allowed. Still, he wouldn't launch the Stinger based on a hairstyle.

"Is it him?" Johnson asked.

"I need to see his face."

"Want me to call him for you?"

"What, you've got his frequency?"

"Don't need it," Johnson said, and he was grinning now. "I've got an air horn."

Bolan smiled and said, "Why not?"

A heartbeat later, the ear-splitting sound echoed over the water, disturbing a few of the swimmers near shore. It reached the submarine and made the solitary figure in the conning tower turn to seek its source.

"It's him," Bolan said, lowering his glasses as he reached down for the Stinger. "Take us in."

LANAKILA WAS SCANNING his target, satisfied that he and his crew had the sea to themselves for the critical moment, when an ungodly blast of noise made him flinch. It sounded like a foghorn, only more high-pitched, and he turned automatically in the direction of the noise, lowering the field glasses that hung around his neck.

He was surprised and mortified to see a cabin cruiser standing off a quarter mile or so from his position, drifting with the tide. Lanakila didn't need his binoculars to know the cruiser's crewmen would be watching him, his hijacked submarine so out of place at Turtle Bay.

Atop the cabin cruiser's flying bridge, one of those crewmen waved an arm above his head and loosed another blare of raucous sound from an air horn.

What did it mean?

Was that a common greeting among boaters, or was he attempting to alert the guests at Turtle Bay? To what? Had word already spread that Pele's Fire had snatched a submarine out of the *haole* Navy's sacred harbor? Was the average pleasure boater on alert for sightings of the *Newark,* or was this man simply drunk and having a good time?

Lanakila raised his binoculars and brought the cabin cruiser into focus. The man on the flying bridge was unkempt, like a *haole* beach bum, but his grin seemed chiseled in ice. It made Lanakila uneasy for reasons he couldn't explain.

He shifted to the cabin cruiser's second passenger, the only other man in evidence aboard. This one was slightly taller, larger than the first, and was surveying Lanakila through his own field glasses. Was it possible for eyes to meet under such circumstances?

Lanakila held his binoculars steady while the stranger lowered his pair, stooped to set it on the deck and rose once more with a long, awkward looking device cradled in his arms.

It couldn't be! A goddamned *Stinger?*

Why would these two *haole* losers on a private pleasure craft have Stinger missiles and—

Forget that shit! Get out of here! a voice in his head cried.

"Not yet," Lanakila told himself, speaking through clenched and grinding teeth. "I have a job to do."

He tugged a walkie-talkie from his belt and thumbed down the transmitter switch. "Fire!" he commanded. "Fire! Fire! Do you hear me? *Fire!*"

"Um, sir," the tinny voice came back, "fire *what?*"

"The Tomahawks, you idiot!"

"How many, sir?"

"All of them! Give the bastards everything we've got!"

"Er, sorry. We can't do that, sir. I mean—"

"Why *can't* you do it? I gave you an order!"

"Yes, sir, but we have to arm and load each one, select the target, and—"

"Well, do it, then! What are you waiting for?"

"Yes, sir, but—"

"Fire the fucking Tomahawks *right now,* or I'll come down

and rip your goddamned heart out of your chest with my bare fucking hands!"

The line went dead between them, and he pictured crewmen racing to obey. Would they be fast enough?

He framed the cabin cruiser in his lenses once again, and saw the stranger with the Stinger missile aiming it directly at the *Newark*. Would it function in those circumstances, when it wasn't pointed at an aircraft?

Lanakila didn't know, and at the moment he was not inclined to test his limited knowledge against the laws of physics. He saw a puff of white smoke from the launcher, and a tail of washed-out orange-and-yellow flame spouting behind it, then the Stinger was racing toward him, faster than God's own chariot on Judgment Day.

Lanakila panicked, dropped his two-way radio and would've lost his field glasses, but for the strap around his sweaty neck. He lunged for the companionway, shouting, "Dive! Dive, goddamnit! Just dive!" at the top of his lungs.

A moment later, he was back in the *Newark*'s command center, his crewmen gaping at him, while he shouted orders with the high-pitched elocution of a manic auctioneer.

"Fire! Dive! Full speed ahead! Dive! Fire!"

His men stood rooted in their tracks, watching their leader come apart before their very eyes. And somewhere in the middle of it, Lanakila suddenly remembered one thing he'd forgotten in his rush to save himself.

He hadn't closed the conning tower's hatch.

BOLAN WAS WATCHING when the Stinger found its target, a direct hit on the *Newark*'s conning tower. Its 3-kilo HE warhead detonated on impact, tearing a ragged vent in the tower that Bolan could see with his binoculars, when the smoke cleared.

Would it be enough to sink the submarine if it submerged? He didn't know and couldn't take that chance.

Johnson had the *China Girl* in motion, veering toward the

sub and accelerating to the limit of its twin-engine power. Ashore, the air horn and missile explosion had roused some of the sunbathers from their torpor, focusing eyes out to sea where the battle was joined.

Bolan shouldered one of the three Russian RPG-7s, waiting for Johnson to close within the tank-killer's effective range. He didn't think that the rocket-propelled grenades could pierce the sub's hull, but if they hit the Stinger's point of impact, or close enough to it, they might do some serious damage.

A long shot, maybe.

But it was the only shot he had remaining.

Bolan didn't shout at Johnson to increase the cabin cruiser's speed. He was already doing what he could and holding nothing back. Machines could only do so much. The one that failed first might determine who emerged victorious this day, and who became fish food.

Three hundred yards.

Bolan stood ready with the RPG. Its twenty-five pounds felt like nothing, barely there. Wood wrapped around the middle of the milled-steel tube would insulate his shoulder from the heat of the initial blast. The projectile's rocket motor would ignite some thirty feet downrange, propelling it toward impact with the target.

Ready.

Bolan braced himself, although the RPG produced no significant recoil. The cabin cruiser's motion could throw off his aim, unless he made adjustments and controlled the launcher.

Aim.

He framed the sub's battered conning tower in the RPG's optical sights, letting Johnson shave another twenty yards off the range while Bolan's index finger curled around the trigger.

Fire!

The RPG's projectile traveled at a rate of 320 yards per second, closing the gap between launcher and target in less than a heartbeat. It found the mark and blew inside the cavity created by the Stinger's high-explosive warhead moments earlier. This time, Bolan saw flames, and white smoke poured out of the *Newark*'s jagged wound.

Again, he thought, and reached down for the second RPG. He shouldered it, sighted as Johnson slowed the cabin cruiser to avoid ramming the submarine and fired again. Another rocket found its target, vanished through the ragged hole, then detonated in a smoky thunderclap.

The submarine was moving forward now and settling lower in the water. Bolan feared he was about to lose his chance and grabbed the final RPG, sighting and firing almost in a single fluid movement. There was no surprise at the explosion, this time, only a vague sense of pity for the men inside the *Newark*.

Were they doomed?

He didn't know.

The sub had power and was capable of surface navigation, at the very least. Whether its crewmen had the will or the ability to dive, was something else entirely.

And they did.

Crouched and reaching for his first LAW rocket, Bolan saw the *Newark* sinking out of sight. There could be no mistake about it. He had no time for a parting shot, before the hijacked vessel disappeared below the waves.

"What do you think?" Johnson asked, from the flying bridge, then answered his own question. "Jesus, I don't know. It could go either way."

It could, thought Bolan. But it won't.

LANAKILA WAS RUSHING toward the companionway when another explosion rocked the sub. Smoke erupted from the conning tower overhead, some of it boiling down into the command room, while wind swept the rest away from the ship.

Lanakila's ears were still numb from the first blast, but he felt something whistling past him, heard muted sounds around him as the shards of twisted steel struck bulkheads, furniture and instruments. One of his men cried out and fell, clutching a thigh that spouted blood between his fingers.

Behind him, someone shouted, "Dive! Dive! Dive!"

He turned to bellow, *"Wait!"* before another blast ripped through the conning tower, driving Lanakila to his knees. This time, a piece of shrapnel drew a line of fire across his scalp and sent blood spilling warm into his eyes.

Panicked and dazed, Lanakila staggered to his feet. Only the tower's gaping hatch meant anything to him right now. He didn't know or care if the explosions meant the submarine had other fatal leaks. He only wanted to eliminate the one that was his fault.

To die, if that was in the cards for him today, knowing it wasn't due to his stupid mistake.

Lanakila stepped onto the bottom rung of the companionway, reached up to grasp the rungs above him, climbing into bitter smoke. He felt the *Newark* tilting forward, diving in accordance with his last clear order.

Plunging forward to destruction.

Out of nowhere, fragments of an ancient movie flashed across Lanakila's mind. Something he'd seen when he was just a kid, with German subtitles that left him frustrated, about a German U-boat during one of the world wars. He still recalled the way that movie boat had come apart and drowned a number of its crew when depth charges were going off around it.

Now, that gruesome end seemed destined to be his, unless…

He made one last try for the hatch, and yet another thunderous explosion knocked him sprawling. Deafened even to his own fierce curses, Lanakila struggled to all fours, using the long sleeve of his poopy suit to wipe blood from his eyes.

A gush of seawater descended from the conning tower's open hatch, or maybe through a hole made by the rocket blasts. Salt water blinded Lanakila, stung his ragged scalp wound, but it also helped revive him. This would be his absolute last chance to save himself, his crew and the main event.

"Surface!" he shouted at his men in the command center. "Surface and fire the Tomahawks!"

They gaped at him as if he were insane, but the deluge of seawater apparently convinced them that submerging would be tantamount to suicide. Two of them started grappling with the submarine's controls, while the third lay barely moving, still clutching his wounded leg, but lying in a foot of brackish, bloodstained water now.

Since neither Lanakila's throttleman nor planesman had relayed his firing order to the weapons center, he sloshed through calf-deep seawater to reach the intercom. He keyed it and began to speak without preamble.

"Fire those Tomahawks! As many as you can! We must destroy the target and our enemies! Acknowledge!"

An eternal second later, a familiar voice came back to him from far away. "Fire Tomahawks. Yes, sir. We're still…we're trying…we—"

"Just *do it!*" Lanakila raged, wishing that he could reach out through the intercom and wrap his hands around the lazy little weasel's neck. "Do it, goddamn you! Fire those fucking missiles!"

But instead of a response, he heard two distant voices arguing. They came out of the speaker mounted near his head, but Lanakila found he couldn't interrupt them with new orders, couldn't tell them to quit squabbling like children and get on with it. His thumb on the transmit button had no effect.

Now, what the hell?

He guessed that seawater had shorted out the system, somehow, and the intercom was locked on Send at their end of the line. Lanakila leaned in closer, water nearly to his knees now, even though they had resurfaced, eavesdropping and trying to make sense of what he heard.

"That's not the way you—"

"I know how to load the fucking—"

"Do it right, then, will you?"

"This *is* right!"

"It's *backward,* you dumb shi—"

A bone-deep shudder rocked the *Newark,* nearly toppling Lanakila off his feet. He clutched the periscope to stay upright, standing with eyes closed, shoulders slumped in grim defeat.

Too late, he thought. Too fucking late.

"WE LOST HER, damn it," Johnson said from the cabin cruiser's flying bridge. "Good shooting, but she's gone."

"I'm not so sure," Bolan replied.

"Come on, bro. Everybody on the beach, there, saw the fireworks. In fifteen, twenty minutes, we'll have half a dozen Coast Guard cutters climbing up our ass, and never mind the Navy. If we don't split now, we may not have another chance."

Bolan could not dispute the surfer-mercenary's logic, but he answered, "Wait a bit."

"How long's a bit?" Johnson asked.

"Not too long."

"Well, since you're being all precise and everything…okay."

Bolan stood still and watched the foaming water where the *Newark* had submerged a moment earlier. Less than a minute passed, and maybe less than half that, when the sea downrange appeared to swell once more, the dark form of the fast-attack sub rising from the green Pacific depths.

"Jesus, they're back," Johnson said. "How in hell did you know—?"

"Not important now," Bolan replied. "Get after them."

"Say what?"

"We have to finish it!"

"With what, man? Small-arms fire? Maybe you want to try a spear gun on that fish?"

"I've got the LAWs," Bolan reminded him.

"All right, for Christ's sake! Here we go. Sink that bitch this time."

Smiling, Bolan picked up the first LAW rocket launcher, as Johnson gunned the *China Girl*'s twin engines. The cabin cruiser lurched forward, snarling in pursuit of the *Newark,* while the submarine ran on the surface.

By submerging, Lanakila's crew had doused the fire inside the punctured conning tower. Bolan didn't know if there'd been any flooding belowdecks, but he could see the U-boat was still up and running, so it wasn't finished yet.

The LAWs would pack a relatively weak punch, when compared with what he'd fired against the submarine so far, but they were all he had, aside from small arms lined up on the deck. The Stoner LMG and other weapons would be useful only if the *Newark*'s crew came out on deck, where he could pick them off. Until then—

Bolan wasn't sure what happened next.

He had been lining up his first LAW round, waiting for Johnson to present him with a clear shot at the conning tower, when the whole sub seemed to lurch or jump somehow. It didn't come out of the water, nothing so dramatic, but there was a mighty shudder, followed by—

A hundred feet or so behind the conning tower, an explosion dwarfing anything that Bolan's RPGs or Stinger might have caused, a fireball riding peals of thunder shot up through the *Newark*'s afterdeck. Large chunks of twisted, blackened steel were airborne, slicing through a mushroom cloud of smoke that issued from somewhere inside the boat.

"Jesus, Joseph and Mary!" Johnson swore. "Did you do that?"

"I don't see how I—"

Bolan's answer was eclipsed and smothered by the next blast, and the next, until they started slamming *Newark* like a string of giant firecrackers exploding in the big sub's passageways and living quarters. Bolan lowered his LAW rocket launcher, stood and watched the U-boat self-destruct.

Once it began, the process was both swift and irreversible. The first blast had erupted from amidships, but they ran in both directions after that, shredding the *Newark*'s decks and hull from bow to stern. The conning tower lifted off, at one point, rose a hundred feet or so into the air then tumbled back into the sea, a smoking heap of scrap metal.

There was no question of survivors. Bolan didn't know how many men had followed Lanakila on his final one-way ride. No one might ever verify their names, under the circumstances. He felt sorry for them, in the abstract, trapped inside the submarine during its fiery death throes, but his grudging sympathy could not have been confused with mourning.

Lanakila and his followers had set their own course for disaster. They'd intended it to fall on others, killing hundreds— even thousands—with the *Newark*'s Tomahawks, but they had failed. The plan had, literally, blown up in their faces.

How?

Bolan supposed that Brognola might have an answer for him later, when the Navy experts had retrieved whatever wreckage they could find, formed their committees, analyzed the evidence. Congress would likely get in on the act, hold hearings, let the politicians grab their photo ops and strike their postures of concern. If any truth came out of that, Bolan would file it in his mental database for future reference.

In case he ever had to kill another submarine.

"I'd say we're finished now," Johnson called down from the flying bridge.

"I'd say."

"Okay to take this baby back to port, then?"

"Anytime you're ready, Captain."

"Argh, me hearties!" Johnson growled and cackled. "We should fly a Jolly Roger, next time out."

"I'm hoping there won't be a next time," Bolan answered, as he started packing up the unused LAWs, grenades and small arms.

"Yeah, I guess that's better, all around. If we can make it past the Coast Guard and whoever, I may have to spend a few more years relaxing on the beach and riding waves."

"It could be worse," Bolan said.

Glancing back toward where the *Newark*'s last remains were sinking out of sight for the last time, Johnson replied, "I hear you, bro. I hear you, loud and clear."

Epilogue

Waialua Bay, Oahu

They had smooth sailing with the *China Girl* on their return from Turtle Bay. En route, Bolan had nearly tossed the Stinger's launcher overboard, but Johnson called down from the flying bridge with a request to save it, pack it with the other weapons going back into his basement stash.

"You have another Stinger?" Bolan asked him.

"Not yet," Johnson answered, grinning, "but you never know what's going to be offered at a North Shore yard sale."

"Right."

He packed the weapons, stowed their cases out of sight be-lowdecks, just in case they should be stopped and questioned, but the federal boats Bolan was watching for never appeared.

Maybe they'd come at Turtle Bay around the north end of the island, he decided. Or, they might have been distracted searching for the *Newark* south of Pearl. In any case, the word would definitely spread from Turtle Bay by telephone, e-mail, what-have-you. With so many politicians and celebrities in residence at the resort, he would've been surprised if someone hadn't called the Pentagon already to report the offshore battle.

Bolan hoped that no one with binoculars could name the *China Girl*, but that would soon be someone else's problem. Even if the boat was traced, its owner would be solid with an airtight alibi—or, maybe Johnson could supply one for his friend, if there was any doubt.

Bolan had no fear that the surfer-merc might rat him out, even if Johnson was detained for questioning. They'd graduated from the same hard school, although in different classes, and the rules were absolute.

As for the others, Leia Aolani and Mano Polunu, they had seen his face but didn't know his name, could tell the Feds nothing of any substance if they found themselves caged in interrogation rooms. Bolan doubted that that would happen, but his trail was covered, just in case.

A few more hours, and he would be gone.

A phantom, up in smoke.

The *China Girl* nosed into Waialua Bay without mishap. As they approached its berth, Bolan saw Aolani sitting on the pier. She scrambled to her feet as they approached, looking particularly anxious as she caught the mooring lines that Bolan tossed out from the cabin cruiser's deck.

"What happened?" she asked Bolan.

Bolan countered with a question of his own. "Where's Polunu?"

"He took off," she said. "Well, actually, I drove him back to Haleiwa. When I left him, he was waiting for a bus."

"To where?"

"He didn't say. I didn't ask."

Johnson stepped onto the pier, and Aolani gave a little running hop into his arms. The surfer looked surprised, but pleasantly, and didn't argue when she kissed him on the lips.

"Are you all right?" she asked.

"No damage to report, ma'am."

Aolani took a long step backward, then asked both of them at once, "What happened? Tell me everything. There's nothing on the radio, so far. Did you—?"

"It's done," Bolan replied. "I don't know what the media will have to say about it, but the main event is canceled."

"So, we won!" Aolani said.

Bolan offered no response to that. In his experience, while

enemies could certainly be killed and buried, predators as a generic breed were indestructible. Kill one, ten, or a hundred, and more rushed to fill the empty slots. They might not share the same philosophy, religion—name your poison—but their tactics wouldn't change beyond adoption of the latest megakill technology.

"We won, Sunshine," Johnson said.

Bolan and Johnson started hauling bags of military hardware from the *China Girl,* back to their vehicle.

"You brought back all the guns," Aolani observed, not making it a question.

"What?" Johnson replied. "You thought I planned to throw them overboard?"

"I kept my fingers crossed," she said.

"Not likely," Johnson said. "In case you didn't notice, it's a wild and wacky world out there."

"Maybe we'll work on that," Aolani replied. And smiled.

Honolulu International Airport

AOLANI AND JOHNSON trailed Bolan from Johnson's house back to Honolulu. They waited while Bolan dropped his rental car at the company's satellite office, then chauffeured him to the terminal. Aolani insisted on going in with Bolan, while Johnson went to park his Jeep in the airport's short-term garage.

Bolan was listed as a standby passenger on Continental's next flight to Los Angeles. He wouldn't watch the movie, wouldn't touch the processed food. Instead, he bought a six-pack of expensive bottled "spring water," most likely drawn from someone's kitchen tap in Omaha, Nebraska, or Butte, Montana.

"Anything to read?" Aolani asked, as he left the concourse shop that peddled everything from gum and magazines to baseball caps and cell phone batteries.

"I'll likely sleep most of the way," he said.

"Oh, right. I need to catch up on some beauty rest, myself."

"You'll want to keep your head down for a while," he cautioned.

"Right. Ron mentioned that. Because they weren't all on the...fishing trip."

"Affirmative. Chances are that whoever's left is either scrambling for a place to hide, or else wasn't aware of your part in the game to start with. But you can't be sure."

"I thought it might be better if I had a bodyguard," Aolani said, looking over at Johnson.

Bolan felt a frown tugging the corners of his lips, then saw where she was going with it. "That might be a good idea," he said.

Johnson suddenly appeared at Bolan's elbow. "What sounds like a good idea?" he asked them both.

Aolani flashed a smile. "Never mind. I'll tell you later."

"Should my ears be burning?"

"At the very least," Bolan replied.

They couldn't walk him to the gate. Post-9/11 rules had ended America's long tradition of tearful greetings and send-offs at airport departure or arrival gates. Instead, nonticket holders had to end their journey at the checkpoint where Homeland Security agents, dressed in the black-and-white style of Las Vegas dealers, X-rayed carry-on bags and frisked departing passengers.

"End of the line," Johnson said.

Bolan was grateful for the company *and* for its termination. He had come to do a job, and it was finished. Ron Johnson probably regarded Bolan as a comrade now, their friendship forged in fire, and might agree to help him with some other problem, if their paths should ever cross again by accident.

But Leia Aolani was a different story altogether.

Standing in the airport terminal, with the adventure of a lifetime still fresh in her mind, she may have idealized both Johnson and the man she knew as Matthew Cooper. Maybe they were heroes in her eyes, or something else she couldn't name just now.

But she would find a name for it, someday, and Bolan knew from past experience that violence left a sour aftertaste on most civilized tongues. A week or month from now, she might resent Bolan for answering her own distress call. Might blame him for what she'd seen and done and felt during their short two days together.

"Guess there's no point saying, 'See you soon,' is there?" Johnson asked.

"I doubt it," Bolan said.

"Well, hey, you ever make it back to the North Shore, feel free to look me up. I'll either be here, or I won't."

That grin again, for the last time. Aolani was watching Johnson's face, as if trying to clarify the meaning of his words.

"I will," Bolan said, "if I do."

His words broke Aolani's momentary spell. "Please be careful, Matt," she said.

"My middle name," Bolan replied, and left them standing there together as the line moved forward toward a bulky bald man who was asking everyone to please remove their shoes.

IN FACT, BOLAN DIDN'T sleep the whole way from Oahu to Los Angeles. The standby reservation worked out fine. There were at least two dozen empty seats in coach on Bolan's flight, allowing him to claim a row of three seats for himself. When they were up and well away from Honolulu International, he took the airphone from its cradle on the middle seat in front of him, swiped Matthew Cooper's credit card and dialed a number Brognola answered, day or night.

"Hello."

Brognola's gruff tone on the other end told Bolan that he hadn't been asleep.

"I'm inbound," Bolan said without amenities. "All done, except the mopping up."

"That's what I heard," Brognola said. "Are we secure?"

"Airphone," Bolan replied, which said it all, in terms of

who might eavesdrop on their conversation, either physically or electronically.

"Gotcha. What did you hear before you left?" Brognola asked.

"Nothing. My only information's based on what I saw."

"Okay. My ears say that it may go on the record as an accident. No details yet, but it could smooth things over if they don't get clumsy."

We can always dream, Bolan thought. But he said, "Let's hope they pull it off."

He didn't ask about the body count, how Navy press releases would explain the loss of a nuclear sub with no authorized personnel aboard—or, worse yet, with a renegade crew of civilians.

"Apparently," Brognola said, "it's something of a miracle. Most of the crew escaped unharmed, before the boat went down."

"You said most of the crew?"

"From what I'm hearing, there are six sailors listed as missing from Pearl. Smart money says they'll be the heroes who sacrificed themselves, helping their buddies get to safety. It's sad for the families, of course, but still better than wondering."

Right. And it ties up loose ends, Bolan thought.

Which raised another question in his mind.

"I heard there's been some kind of trouble on the island with a revolutionary group, or something."

"That was the first report," Brognola said. "Turns out that it was gang-related, after all. The cops have found a drug connection. Let me get the name, here…Happy Kiemela, if you can believe it. Seems the so-called revolutionary gang was moving coke, whatever else was readily available. They must've stepped on someone's toes. Likely another dealer, maybe even one of the cartels. My guess would be, the handful who are still alive won't want to talk about it, if they're ever found."

"So, what about this Lanakila character?"

"Looks like he's in the wind," Brognola answered, "with a couple dozen of his chosen people. Everybody's looking for them—DEA, the Bureau, maybe Interpol by now—but no one's giving odds on when or *if* they'll drop the net."

"Some of them may start up again," Bolan said, "when the heat dies down."

"That falls under the heading of somebody else's problem," Brognola replied. "As old J. Edgar used to say, I just report. I don't evaluate."

"Quoting the Hoovermeister," Bolan said. "I never thought I'd hear that."

"Hey, tell me about it. Every morning I get up and shave my father's face. The second childhood can't be far behind."

"Be sure and tell me when it hits," Bolan said. "I can get you half-price tickets for the rides at Disney World."

"Be still, my heart." A silent moment stretched between them, then Brognola asked, "How's everything with you?"

"Couldn't be better," Bolan answered, not quite truthfully.

It could've been *much* better, if his life had taken different turns, back in the day. If Bolan's father hadn't borrowed cash from loan sharks back in Pittsfield, for example. If he hadn't—

Bolan caught himself before that train of thought could leave the station, shut its engine down and turned his back on it.

Memory Lane had highs and lows for Bolan, as it did for everybody. He simply didn't need to take that trip right now.

"You there?" Brognola asked, the man's voice tinny in his ear.

"I'm here."

"Okay. I thought I'd lost you for a second there."

"Not yet."

"For what it's worth," Brognola said, "the Man sends you an attaboy for this one. Does it make you go all warm and fuzzy?"

Bolan smiled, peered out his tiny window at the clouds tinged red and orange by sundown's blaze.

"I wouldn't phrase it quite that way," he answered.

"No. Me, neither. But I had to pass it on."

"Passed and received," Bolan replied.

It was the closest Bolan or the team at Stony Man would ever come to official recognition or praise. None of which mattered to Bolan, since he had never taken a job for a pat on the back.

"So, it's a tragic accident," Brognola said in closing. "I don't get all the technology, but I've been told there was some kind of an explosion inside the sub."

"Any threat to the reactor?" Bolan asked. It had been preying on his mind since he had watched the *Newark* self-destruct. Had they created a long-term disaster in their bid to stop mass murder in the here and now?

"No worries," Brognola assured him. "Nothing nukey for the tourists or the natives to concern themselves about. It's sounding more like some malfunction with the weapons. All strictly conventional."

"So, no Godzilla popping up to step on Honolulu twenty years from now?"

"Only in movie theaters," Brognola said. "Another job well done."

"They'll need to take another look at Pearl's security."

"No doubt. Heads may not roll for this, but they'll be achy when the shouting stops. Still," Brognola admitted, "it could be a whole lot worse."

"The celebration's on, I take it?"

"Should be starting in about…eight hours," Brognola confirmed. "Too bad you have to miss it."

"I already saw the fireworks," Bolan said. "They ought to last me for a while."

"Some R & R will do you good," Brognola said. "Got any special place in mind?"

"Not yet," Bolan replied. "But you know how to reach me."

"That I do. Relax a while. Chill out. Enjoy yourself. You've earned it."

"Maybe," Bolan said. "I'll catch you later."

"Later," Brognola echoed, and broke the link.

Relax. Chill out. Enjoy yourself.

Bolan remembered how to do those things, but he was out of practice. There was always one more job waiting, another predator he had to face.

But not today.

Today, he'd done enough.

As for tomorrow, it would take care of itself.

TAKE 'EM FREE

2 action-packed novels plus a mystery bonus

NO RISK

NO OBLIGATION TO BUY